Yours for Christmas (Maybe)

*She came for her best friend's wedding...
not to fall for the groom's brother.*

Also by Kathryn Kaleigh

The Gravity of Us Series

(Reading Order)

Just Breathe

Just Surface

Just Melt

Standalone Suspense

Out of Ashes

CONTEMPORARY

Alpine Falls (Maybe Yours) Series

(Reading Order)

Still Yours (Maybe)

Yours for Christmas (Maybe)

Forever Yours (Maybe)

(ALPINE FALLS)

Stranded in Alpine Falls

Belonging in Alpine Falls

The Spirit of Christmas in Alpine Falls

Christmas Wishes in Alpine Falls

Finding True North in Alpine Falls

A Ghost of Christmas Magic in Alpine Falls

Secrets and Second Chances

Honeymoon with a Stranger

Not Our Wedding

(SILVER PINES)

The Way Back to You

Back to Where We Began

When We Were Us

(ONCE UPON FOREVER)

My Forever Guy

Our Forever Love

Forever Vows

Finding Forever

Accidentally Forever

(TRUE NORTH)

Borrowed Until Monday

Still Mine

The Moon and the Stars at Christmas

Perfectly Mismatched

On the Way to Forever

A Merry Little Christmas

On the Way Home to Christmas

It was Always You

(UNBREAK MY HEART)

Begin Again

Love Again

Falling Again

(FOR THE LOVE OF THE FLIGHT)

Just Stay

Just Chance

Just Believe

Just Us

Just Once

Just Happened

Just Maybe

Just Pretend

Just Because

(MAGNETIC NORTH)

Second Chance Kisses

Second Chance Secrets

First Time Charm

Three Broken Rules

Second Chance Destiny

Unexpected Vows

(FALLING FOR CHRISTMAS)

The Heart of Christmas

The Magic of Christmas

In a One Horse Open Sleigh

A Secret Royal Christmas

An Old Fashioned Christmas

(CITY SKYLINE BILLIONAIRES)

Billionaire's Unexpected Landing

Billionaire's Accidental Girlfriend

Billionaire's Fallen Angel

Billionaire's Secret Crush

Billionaire's Barefoot Bride

(TRULY, MADLY, DEEPLY)

The Lady in the Red Dress

On the Edge of Chance

Sealed with a Kiss

Kiss Me at Midnight

The Heart Knows

(STOLEN ECHOES)

When Cupid's Arrow Strikes

Chasing Fireflies

A Chance Encounter

(EDGE OF THE HORIZON)

The Forever Equation

Pretend Boyfriend

All our Tomorrows

Kissing for Keeps

Out of the Blue

The Princess and the Playboy

(RED LIPSTICK KISSES)

Red Lipstick Kisses and Small Town Wishes

Stolen Dances and Big City Chances

Chance Connections and Upside Down Plans

A Christmas Kiss on the Twenty-Fifth

Believe in the Magic of Christmas

Vows of Inheritance Series
(Reading Order)

Vow to Protect

Vow to Redeem

ROMANTASY

(IN THE SPIRIT OF LOVE)

Spirits of the Heart

Out of Dreams and Ashes

Etched Upon the Heart

WESTERN ROMANCE

(LONE STAR HEARTS)

Wanted by a Texas Ranger

Saved by a Texas Ranger

(WHISKEY SPRINGS)

Finding Natalie

Promising Samantha

Falling for Allyson

Saving Savannah

Claiming Charlie

Rescuing Keira

Protecting Gabriella

Courting Isabella

TIME TRAVEL

(INTO THE MIST)

Written in the Wind

Scripted in the Stars

Destined in the Twilight

Promised in the Mist

Trapped in the Melody

(DRAGON'S BLOOD)

Dragon's Blood

Lavender Blue

Champagne Silver

Twilight Frost

Mountbatten Pink

(WHEN HEARTSTRINGS BECKON)

Rescued in Time

Meet me in 1879

(WHEN HEARTSTRINGS ECHO)

Messages Across Time

Falling Through to Forever

Once Upon a Winter's Spell

(BECKONED)

Before the Storm

Twist of Fate

When the Stars Align

Once Upon a Christmas

Once in a Blue Moon

A Wish Upon a Star

(BEGUILED)

When Lightning Strikes

Storm of Time

Midnight Storm

When the Moon Falls

Stormborn Angel

(SPELLED)

Time Tempest

The Heart Remembers

A Moment in Time

Moonlight Shadows

HISTORICAL

(TAPESTRY OF BLUE AND GRAY)

Shadows Beneath Magnolia Blooms

Secrets Among Southern Roses

(IT HAPPENED BY ACCIDENT)

Accidentally Alluring

Accidentally Married

(SOUTHERN BELLE CIVIL WAR)

Beyond Enemy Lines

Love Always

Hearts Under Siege

Hearts Under Fire

Away Down South in Dixie

The Reluctant Bride

Stay with Me

Jasmine Kisses

Magnolia Kisses

Gardenia Kisses

(THE QUINNS)

Wait for Me

Take Me Home

Keep Me Safe

FATED MATES

Riley's Mate

Aiden's Mate

Brayden's Mate

STANDALONE SUSPENSE

Lost and Found

All I Want for Christmas

Serenity

Courting Alley Cat

YOURS FOR CHRISTMAS (MAYBE)
PREVIEW — FOREVER YOURS (MAYBE)

Yours for Christmas (Maybe)

THE ALPINE FALLS (MAYBE YOURS) SERIES

KATHRYN KALEIGH

Chapter One

Olivia Harris

"I NEED TO CONFIRM MY RESERVATION." I put the phone on speaker and drop it onto the bed next to my over-stuffed suitcase.

Of course the automated system goes to music. Elevator music. At least it has a Christmas beat to it. So there's that.

Why did Hannah, one of my two best friends, have to get married in winter? In the mountains, no less. She could've had a wedding on a warm beach somewhere like most December brides.

Doesn't she know that packing for a cold weather trip requires ten times as many clothes?

I pull out a chunky, oversized cable sweater that's taking

up a fourth of my whole suitcase and toss it aside. I'll just take it with me. I'll need something warm when I get off the airplane in Denver anyway.

At least now I have room for my maid-of-honor dress. And shoes. I almost forgot my heels.

I dash to the closet and grab the box of sparkly high heels I've only worn once. But they are a perfect match for my new burgundy evening gown with its sparkly waistband.

My dog, a little Yorkshire terrier with an adorable caramel colored head and a white body, trots into the room carrying her leash in her mouth.

She drops it at my feet and barks once.

"Hey Cupcake. Time to go outside?"

Instead of answering, she sits down and looks at me with big puppy dog eyes.

Shoving my phone, still playing nondescript music, into my back pocket, I snap her leash onto her collar and together we head to the back door of my little cottage.

Since I own the house outright after inheriting it from my grandmother, I can have as many dogs living with me as I want to.

Right now I only have Cupcake. I've taken her around to two different families for possible adoption, but they both declined. Something about her fur color not lining up.

It was their loss and since I personally think Cupcake is cute as a bug's ear, I'm keeping her for myself.

The temperature outside is warm. Currently in the seventies. Not like December at all. Cold weather is one point in favor of a mountain wedding. Christmas weather is supposed to be cold.

Cupcake runs down the steps and straight out to her favorite tree where she promptly does her business. Standing at the top of the stairs, I let the leash roll out and somehow she knows exactly when to stop before it runs out and stops. It was a one-trial learning for her to figure out just how far out she could run without her leash running out on her. She has impressive spatial skills in that way.

Not one to dilly dally, Cupcake comes bounding back up the stairs.

I pick her up and carry her the rest of the way inside. Just an excuse to bury my face in her soft fur.

When the doorbell rings, she goes on alert and wiggles until I let her down.

Not expecting anyone, I scowl at the door.

A peek outside tells me its Stan, my current boyfriend. I pick Cupcake up again so she won't run outside and open the door.

"I know," he says, holding up a hand. "I know you're leaving in the morning and don't have time for me tonight, but..." He holds up a paper sack. "I know that you forget to eat."

With a sigh, I open the door. I did forget to eat. Sort of. I got busy packing and didn't bother with it.

He smiles and kisses me on the cheek as he comes inside. "Hello Cupcake," he says to the dog in my arms.

"You're right," I say, taking the bag from him and sliding

two ham sandwiches and two bags of chips out onto the table. "I didn't eat."

"Interesting music," he says.

"What? Oh." I pull my phone out of my back pocket and disconnect the call. "I was trying to confirm my reservation. I'll check online later."

"I brought Cupcake a treat." He pulls a dog treat out of his pocket and Cupcake stands up for it, then runs off to chew on it in private.

"I've decided to keep her," I say, sitting down in one of the wooden chairs at my well-worn square kitchen table that seats four.

"I know," he says.

"How do you know?"

He sits down next to me, unwraps one of the sandwiches and slides it in front of me.

"I know because you like her." He opens a bag of chips. "Besides. You need a dog."

"A pet makes a house a home," I say with a sigh. It's the tagline on our pet adoption agency website.

My two friends, Hanna (the one who ran off to Colorado and is getting married) and Madison and I have our own pet adoption agency. When we started Madison and I were handling the dogs while Hanna was handling cat adoptions.

But now that Hanna is in Colorado, we all do what we can. Quite truthfully, Hanna isn't doing much pet adoption work at all. She lives in a tiny little mountain town and helps her husband/fiancé's family with their horse ranch. Yes. Her relationship is complicated. Long story. She was married, but thought she was divorced for ten years. So they're getting married again.

"Are you sure I can't go with you?" Stan asks.

"You've got finals to grade and two grad student dissertations to chair," I say. "And your sister is coming in from Portugal for Christmas."

"I know. I was hoping you'd be here to spend some time with her."

I smile. "Maybe later." It's about as noncommittal as I can get.

I like Stan. He's a good guy. Thoughtful. Dependable. Always thinking about me.

Is there a spark? Define spark.

He knows, should know, because I've told him, that I don't want to get married. It's not him. It's me. I like being single.

"It's okay," he says. "You need to be with your friend. Maybe my sister will be still be in country when you get back."

"Maybe," I say with a forced smile before I bite into the sandwich.

"Are you sure you don't want me to keep Cupcake for you?"

"That would be the sane thing to do. But no. Cupcake is coming with me."

"When you adopt, you go all in, don't you?"

"You know I do. That's why I try to get the dogs — and cats — out of here as soon as I can. I get attached."

He grins. I try not to roll my eyes. I know exactly what he's thinking. He's thinking that I must surely be getting attached to him by now. We've been seeing each other since spring.

It's impossible not to like Stan. It's also almost impossible to keep him from getting his hopes up that we're ever going to be something we're not.

Chapter Two

Olivia

Shortly after landing at the Denver airport, I discover that the car rental agencies were not prepared for the number of people heading into the mountains for the holidays.

It makes no sense to me. Hannah warned me that Alpine Falls and Whiskey Springs and a couple of the other little towns like Silver Pines, are Christmas destinations.

Every year.

If I was managing a car rental agency, I would make sure to have enough cars on hand for this time of year. Most especially enough cars to cover the reservations.

But they don't. I send Hannah a text.

> I'm in Denver. But there are no cars.

HANNAH

> Somehow not surprised.

> Options?

HANNAH

> I'll come get you.

I've already studied the map in preparation for my drive. It's a good three hour drive up to Alpine Falls. Then she'd have to drive here, then back into the mountains. At least six hours for her. Plus I have to wait here for her.

> No. Let me think.

I do a quick online search.

> I'll get a car to the train station and ride the train up there.

Thought bubbles.
Then nothing.
I shift the pet carrier on my shoulder. Cupcake is getting heavy.
I sit down on a bench and look for an Uber.

HANNAH

> We have a better solution. Jack's brother is in Denver. He can swing by the airport and pick you up.

> Jack's brother?

HANNAH

Trenton

So Trenton Thompson. I vaguely remember Hannah mentioning that Jack had a couple of brothers. I know absolutely nothing about them.

But. I like the idea of hitching a ride far better than I like the idea of sitting here for three plus hours waiting for Hannah to get here or worse, riding a train.

I had enough trouble with airplane staff leaving me alone about Cupcake. The thought of going through that again to try to get Cupcake on a train is daunting at best.

Speaking of Cupcake, she needs to go outside for a potty break.

Okay. I'll go outside and wait.

HANNAH

Can't you wait inside the airport?

I can. But I have to take Cupcake for a bathroom break.

HANNAH

Oh. Okay. Let me get in touch with Trenton.

I stare at the people hurrying past. Something about being in an airport makes people feel like they have to rush from one place to the next. It's part of the energy that comes with being here.

So this guy, Trenton, doesn't know he's giving me a ride.

Isn't that just great.

After I take my dog outside for a walk, I'll read up on the train. It might end up being my best option after all.

I hoist Cupcake's carrier back over my shoulder and, dragging my overstuffed suitcase along behind me, head for the nearest door to the outside world. If I ran an airport, I'd put in a park where people could walk their dogs. But, of course, that isn't going to happen.

Chapter Three

Trenton Thompson

My meeting went well. I'm not sure why the meeting had to be in Denver. I think the owners of the little company were trying to impress people with their fancy meeting space and city attorneys sitting at the table.

If I get the job, great. If I don't, that's okay, too.

Either way, my building design is solid and they'd be crazy to walk away from it. If they walk away, I'll use the ideas in my next projects. Sure. I'll only be able to use bits and pieces for the next client. Each client has their own unique needs.

As an architect, I pride myself on listening to what a

client wants, hearing what they need, and putting it all together into something they can be proud of.

I'm back in my car before I turn my phone back on. I learned the hard way that the phone has to actually be turned off during presentations. Otherwise, even a phone on silent is a distraction.

When my father fell from a horse and had to be rushed to the hospital, I'd had my phone on silent. Keeping my focus on the presentation while watching those texts come through had been brutal. If I could rewind time, I'd probably stop my presentation and go to my family. At the time, however, I'd been determined to land the contract on the table in front of me. I'd done it, too. No one had ever suspected what I'd been going through. Fortunately it all turned out well with my father. But things could have gone badly in so many different ways.

I have a string of messages from my brother, Jack.

Jack is getting married in a couple of weeks. Married to the girl he's been secretly married to for ten years. Long story. He didn't sign the divorce papers. She thought he had.

They're doing the right thing renewing their vows in a small ceremony.

Small, but Hannah's two friends are going to be there. One of them, Olivia, is apparently already on her way here.

And she's stuck at the airport with no rental car. Typical. There are never enough rental cars.

I send my brother a message.

> Why don't you just fly down and
> pick her up?

My brother is a pilot with his own small jet. He literally could just fly down and fly Olivia back up to Alpine Falls.

JACK

Because I'm out on a trail ride
with eight guests.

Right. Of course. My brother Jack is running the ranch while our father is off his feet. I have a feeling that Jack and his wife are going to continue to run the ranch from here on out. Our parents are getting up in age and running a horse ranch is brutally hard work.

Makes sense.

JACK

Just swing by the airport and pick
her up.

I'm on the other side of town.

JACK

She's waiting. Her name is Olivia.

Olivia. Yes. I know. I read your
other ten messages.

JACK

Thanks Bro.

Sometimes having a family is a pain in the ass. This is exactly why I live in Boulder. It's just close enough to my family that I can visit, but I don't have to be involved in their day-to-day lives.

Living too close and things like this happens.

And apparently things like this happen anyway.

Not really having a choice about picking up Olivia from the airport, I buckle up and back out of the parking spot. I can't very well leave a young lady stranded at the airport.

Being a gentleman has been pounded into me since I was a boy. My mother raised her three boys with an iron fist and made sure we understood how to treat women.

Traffic is brutal, as always. I turn on the radio and make the best of it. Christmas music on every channel. I try not to be a scrooge, but by Thanksgiving, I'm pretty much sick of all the Christmas festivities.

As the airport comes into sight, I realize I don't know what Olivia looks like. How am I supposed to find this woman when I don't know what she looks like?

I send my brother a message, but his phone is obviously out of range.

I'm on my own on this one.

After making it to the airport, I watch as a large commercial airplane takes off practically right over the road. With my brother being a pilot, I've spent my share of time at airports, but unlike Jack, I don't have that draw to airplanes. Feeling the allure of the sky is something I can appreciate, but never share with Jack.

Instead of parking in the parking lot, I pull up to the main doors.

A woman comes out the doors, walking a little dog. The dog, a Yorkshire terrier, if I know my dogs, is rather odd looking. Cute, but odd. The woman is... actually quite stunning. She has a sassy short bob of blonde hair that just barely brushes her shoulders. She's wearing a chunky sweater over jeans and sneakers on her feet. Casual but with an urban vibe about her.

She's holding the dog's leash with one hand and pulling her suitcase with the other, a pet carrier secured to the top of the suitcase. She carries a computer bag on one shoulder and an oversized handbag on the other, balancing it all with surprising grace.

But, seriously, who brings a dog to an airport?

Since I can't leave my car, I get out and lean against the hood. Maybe someone had the good sense to send Olivia a description of me or even what kind of car I drive. Either would be helpful.

I send my brother another text.

> Would help if I had her number.

After a few minutes, the woman walks back this way, picks up her dog and sits on a bench with it in her lap. I cross my arms and keep my eyes open for someone who looks like she might be waiting for a ride.

Maybe I should just park the car and go inside to look for Olivia.

I glare at my phone.

Try sending Hannah a message, but her phone is out of range also.

Why did no one think to send me Olivia's number?

I scroll back through my previous messages, but I definitely don't have her number.

A few people come out the door, but none of them look like a woman heading to Alpine Falls. I try to imagine what a friend of Hannah's might look like.

Hannah is thin and casual-looking, but then Hannah is different because she's actually from Alpine Falls. Her friend won't be from Alpine Falls. Her friend will be from Houston.

My gaze strays back to the young lady sitting with the dog. She's also typing on her own phone and not looking too happy.

I need a sign. That's what people do in the movies.

Annoyed with myself that I didn't already think of that, I climb back in my car and write *Olivia* in big letters on a blank piece of paper.

Taking my sign, I go back to my station near the hood of the car. Now I'm feeling pretty much like a dumbass standing here holding a sign.

Jack and Hannah owe me big time.

Chapter Four

Olivia

> HANNAH
>
> Trenton is coming to pick you up.

I WALK outside the front doors of the airport. The air out here smells like exhaust. And not only that, the air is dry. I can tell as soon as I step outside that the air is different. Hannah told me to bring moisturizer and now I understand why.

There are cars lined up, waiting for people. Dropping people off. Typical airport.

Not seeing any grass anywhere where Cupcake can take her potty break, I find a private space with a little patch of rocks and after making sure Cupcake's harness is secure, lift her out of the carrier to do her business.

Since she was cramped up in the carrier for so long, I keep her leash short and walk around with her some, letting her get some exercise. It's not like we're going anywhere right now.

My stomach growls and I realize it's mid-afternoon and I haven't eaten anything all day. Thanks to Stan, I ate last night, so I can make it to Alpine Falls. Maybe. If I ever get there.

I sit down on a bench, happy to take from break from the weight of my computer bag and purse from my shoulders.

A man pulls up in a new sedan, gets out of his car, and leans against the hood.

He most definitely does not look like someone from Alpine Falls. Not that Jack did either when I'd seen him in Houston a few months ago.

The guy leaning on the car looks like a guy out one of those men's magazines. Perfect hair and perfect business suit. Definitely not from Alpine Falls.

Gathering Cupcake up into my lap, I send Hannah a message.

How am I supposed to find Trenton?

No response. It doesn't even look like it's been delivered. Great. The train is sounding better and better.

The magazine guy gets back into his car. I study the train

schedules. The last train leaves in... I glance at the time... thirty minutes.

Well. So much for that. My next option is to get a hotel room and try again tomorrow.

If there still aren't any rental cars, which I am almost certain if there were no cars today when I actually had a reservation, there's no way I'll get a car tomorrow when I don't have one, I can at least get on the train. Or maybe I'm going to have to let Hannah come and pick me up after all.

Now I'm thinking crazy thoughts like maybe I should have let Stan come along. Not that Stan could have produced a rental car, but this whole ordeal would seem less daunting with someone else along.

And if I'm quite honest with myself, that's probably the main reason I keep Stan around. To have someone to do things with. Maybe it's not the best reason, but it seems like as good a reason as any all things considered in this world we live in.

Stan is dependable and safe. That's not easy to find in someone these days, at least not in my experience.

The handsome magazine guy gets out of his car and, leaning on his hood again, holds up a piece of paper. A sign?

I squint in his direction. It looks like he's holding up a sign. It's too far away, of course, for me to read it.

A sign would have been a good idea. People do that in the movies all the time. It's how strangers find each other at the airport.

It suddenly occurs to me that I need a sign. I need a sign

that reads *Trenton*. That way when he drives up, he'll know I'm waiting for him.

Of course, I have no paper. An iPad, but no paper. Maybe I can make a sign on my iPad.

Or... I get up, set Cupcake on her feet, and after gathering up all my things, securing my handbag and computer bag over my shoulder, grabbing the handle of my suitcase with my other hand, and walk over to the man. If a man has a sheet of paper, he'll have more than one. It's some kind of law.

"Hi," I say, smiling at him.

"Hi." He looks a little startled that I'm talking to him.

"I'm sorry to bother you, but I was wondering if maybe I could borrow a sheet of paper."

"Okay," he says, but doesn't move.

"I'm supposed to be meeting someone, but I don't know him and I need to make a sign."

"Sure." Now he seems a little annoyed. Oh well. "Hold this." He thrusts his own sign into my hands and opens up his car door.

I glance down at the sign.

Olivia.

Chapter Five

Trenton

I'm leaning into the back seat of my car, digging in my briefcase for a sheet of paper when the woman with the dog says "Never mind."

I back out of the car, straighten and look at her. "So now you don't need any paper?"

"I won't be needing to make a sign after all," she says, biting my bottom lip.

"Okay," I say, closing the car door. "Fine by me."

She holds up my sign. "Olivia," she says.

"That's who I'm waiting for."

"I'm Olivia," she says as though I'm the stupidest person she ever met.

I glance down at her dog, then back up to look more closely at her. She has forest green eyes framed with thick dark lashes.

My gaze snags on her plump, kissable lips curved into a little amused smile.

"You're Olivia? Hannah's friend?"

"Yes. Are you Jack's brother?"

I take a deep breath. Let it out slowly. "Yes."

"What's your name?" she asks, suddenly suspicious.

"Trenton." She looks at me with one eyebrow lifted. "Thompson."

She seems satisfied with that. "I think you're my ride."

"You're headed to Alpine Falls?" I try to keep the disbelief out of my voice.

"Yes."

"Okay. Let's go."

I pop the trunk and after she drags her suitcase around, I grab it up and toss it in. It weighs a ton.

"This is Cupcake," she says.

"You brought a dog on an airplane?" I ask.

"Yes," she says somewhat defensively.

"I didn't know that was allowed."

"It's allowed. But. I don't think people like it very much."

"I wouldn't think so."

"You don't like dogs?"

"I like dogs fine. I just didn't know they were allowed on airplanes."

"I guess I lucked out and got a lenient crew."

"Cupcake needs to ride in her carrier," I say, opening the back door and taking her computer bag to stash it in on the seat.

"Why?"

"Safety. And it's the law." I honestly don't know if it's the law or not, but even if it's not, it should be.

"Okay." She secures the dog in the carrier and sets it on the back seat. "Do you want me to ride in the back, too?"

"Why would you do that?"

"I don't know," she says. "You just don't seem very friendly."

I open the passenger door and hold it while she climbs inside. She's absolutely right. I'm not being very friendly. I've been annoyed by the whole ordeal. Not exactly the way to welcome one of my sister-in-law's friends.

"Please accept my apology," I say before I close the passenger door, not waiting for an answer.

This woman reminds me of my mother. She doesn't seem like one to put up with bullshit.

I walk around and get into the driver's seat.

"How was your flight?" I ask as I buckle up and start the motor.

"Fine," she says.

"You must be hungry."

"A little."

"When was the last time you ate?"

"I ate last night."

"That's too long to go without eating," I say.

"You sound like my... friend."

"Hannah?"

"No. A different friend." She looks away.

"We'll stop and get something to eat before we leave the city. Can't have you going hungry."

"I'll be okay."

"I have no doubt about that, but as your welcoming committee, it's my job to make sure you're taken care of."

"Welcoming committee?" she asks with clear skepticism.

"I thought I apologized for not being friendly."

"You did. I'm just not sure I forgive you yet."

With a smile, I get us onto the interstate. This girl might be odd enough to bring a dog with her to an airport, but she's also entertaining.

Chapter Six

Hannah

JACK'S BROTHER is nothing like I expected. Although he's good looking, he doesn't look like Jack. Of course I only saw Jack that one time and only briefly, so I could easily be missing the resemblance.

He's also a bit of a smartass and not very friendly.

And although he claims he likes dogs, I'm not so sure I believe him.

All in all, Trenton comes across as quite disagreeable.

On the interstate now, it looks like we're going to be stuck in traffic.

"Not the best time to be driving in the city," he says.

"Is there ever a good time?"

"In Denver? Not really? It seems like rush hour is all the time."

"It's not quite that bad in Houston."

He changes the channel on the radio. Then changes it again.

"Nothing but Christmas music," he says.

"What's wrong with Christmas music? It's almost Christmas."

He changes the channel again. More Christmas music. "It's been almost Christmas for a month now. Don't people get tired of hearing the same old songs over and over?"

"I don't know. I play my favorite songs over and over again. I don't get tired of them."

"I guess you have a point."

We pass by a pickup truck with a freshly-cut Christmas tree secured in the truck bed.

I turn back to Trenton. "Are you one of those people who doesn't like Christmas?"

"I didn't say I didn't like Christmas. I just get tired of the hype. We barely get into November and everything is all about Christmas. Normal business practically shuts down for weeks. Then after that one day gets here, it's all over. All that hype for that one day."

"So why don't you tell me how you really feel?"

He glances over at me with a perplexed expression, then smiles.

"I guess you're one of those people who loves the holidays."

"What's not to love? There's an energy in the air that isn't there any other time."

"I guess so," he says. "It just makes it hard to conduct any business."

I tuck my hair behind my ears and turn my gaze back to the traffic. We're heading west, toward the snow-capped mountains. Having never been to the mountains, I'm finding the prospect of finally getting to be in the high elevation a little exciting.

"What kind of work do you do?" I ask.

"I'm an architect."

"Oh." I nod and keep my thoughts to myself. It seems to me like any kind of architectural work could easily wait until after Christmas.

"You don't think my work is important," he says.

I look at him with a vexed expression. "I did not say that. I'm sure what you do is very important."

"There are people who want to move forward with their building plans during the holidays but can't because everything slows down."

"Doesn't building slow down in the winter anyway? What with the rain and, up here, the snow?"

"Sure. But mostly just for the external part of the buildings. Work on the interiors continues."

"You do interior work?"

"I'd say that's the bulk of what I do."

"Oh. Well. I'm sorry your work slows down in December."

"What about yours? What do you do?"

"Pet adoptions. We usually see an upswing. But not so much this year."

"People want pets for Christmas." I can't tell if he's being sarcastic or not. "What's different this year?"

"I don't know. I think it's our focus. With Hannah moving up here and getting married, it's splintered our company."

He changes lanes and we're able to speed up for a bit.

"You do know that Hannah is already married, right?"

"Oh no," I say, shaking my head.

"Oh no what?"

"Don't tell me you not only don't like Christmas, but you don't believe in romance either?"

"I didn't say that. There's a little diner about a mile up ahead."

"Okay. I guess since it's not hot outside, Cupcake can stay in the car, but I need to feed her, too."

"Sure." He exits and finds a parking space near the door. "Wait here for a minute," he says. "I need to check on something."

"Sure." Wondering what he could possibly have to check on, I watch him go inside the little diner. Maybe he's checking to see if they have any tables.

I check my phone for messages. Still nothing from Hannah.

Not wanting to keep sending unanswered messages, I don't tell her I found Trenton and that I'm on my way. She'll find out soon enough.

Trenton comes back to the car. "I spoke to the manager," he says. "You can bring Cupcake inside."

"Oh. Okay." I did not expect that. It's the first really kind thing he's done since I met him.

Maybe he isn't so bad as I initially thought after all.

Chapter Seven

Trenton

THE HOSTESS USHERS us to a booth in the back of the diner.

It's just a little diner in two old train cars put together, very retro and very architecturally creative. Someone took one of the long walls off each of the two cars and then welded them together. Worn maroon colored leather seats at the dozen or so booths. Metal stools with matching seat covers at the bar.

Christmas music plays in the background, but it's old music from early last century. It fits the diner and doesn't bother me.

The cook is hard at work at the grill. Everything here is

fried. I don't think they bake anything, except maybe the apple pies that are impossible to resist. I usually get a whole pie to go when I'm headed to Alpine Falls and just a slice if I'm heading home to Boulder. This is a whole apple pie day.

The diner is one of my regular stops on trip from Denver into the mountains. I was first drawn to it because of its creative use of a couple of old train cars, but then I discovered its excellent food and eventually became friends with the staff. Some would call me a regular even though sometimes I go weeks without stopping in.

We borrow a couple of bowls, one for water and one for food, and set Cupcake up a place on the floor beneath our table to eat. While Cupcake devours her food, Olivia checks out the Christmas tree that just so happens to be next to our booth.

"Look at how cute this tree is," she says. "All the decorations are little dogs and even a few cats. So sweet."

Alice, the waitress, comes to our table to take our order.

"Can I get you something to drink?" she asks.

"Just water," Olivia says. "I love your tree."

"Thanks," Alice says, smiling. "It was my idea."

"And it was a wonderful idea," Olivia says.

"I'll be right back with your water and a coke for you Trenton."

Olivia sits down at the booth and looks at me.

"Come here often?" she asks.

I smile at her way of asking how I know the staff. "Whenever I'm down this way."

"Well. Cupcake likes it here."

"If Cupcake likes it, that's saying something."

She tilts her head as she looks at me. She can't tell if I'm being sincere or smartassed and quite frankly I'm not sure which way I'm leaning at the moment.

I'm still getting over being annoyed at having been strong-armed into giving this woman and her dog a ride to Alpine Falls.

The problem with my annoyance is that I'm struggling to hold onto it. Olivia is actually a delight to be around and Cupcake is weirdly cute in her own way.

Alice quickly brings Olivia's water and my coke to the table.

"Need some time to look at the menu?" she asks, holding a little pad and pencil at the ready.

"Yes, please," Olivia says. "What's good?"

"Everything," Alice says, then looks at me. "Don't let her leave without apple pie."

"Wouldn't think of it," I say. "In fact, I'm heading to Alpine Falls, so save me a couple back."

"Consider it done," Alice says. "I'll be back in five to take your order."

"What do you like?" I ask, sliding a menu over to Olivia.

She opens it up and studies it. I fully expect her to order a salad, maybe the chicken salad. Something light. Dressing on the side.

After a quick perusal of the menu, she sets it aside.

"Find anything to your liking?" I ask.

"I think I'll have the ham sandwich with fries."

"Good choice," I say, trying to hide my surprise that she would order something so robust. "I'll have the same."

Cupcake finishes her meal and Olivia puts her on the seat next to her. The dog curls up and goes to sleep. The dog being so well behaved surprises me, too.

"I want to get a photo of the Christmas tree," she says. "For our website. Do you think they would mind?"

"I don't know why they would."

She pulls out her phone and proceeds to photograph the Christmas tree with pet decorations.

Alice takes our order. "I'll have it right out."

Sitting back down, she zooms in on one of the photos and holds it up for me to see. "Look. Some of the lights are even shaped like dogs. Where do you think they found something like that?"

"I wouldn't know. We can ask."

I don't dislike Christmas. Not exactly anyway. It's more like I tolerate it.

I've never had one of those magical Christmasses like they show in the movies where everything comes together. Sure. I enjoy the time spent with my family. The food. The football games. Even the presents are sometimes fun, but as for magic, not so much.

This year, the focus is going to be on Hannah and Jack, as it should be since they're getting married (again) on Christmas Eve. Apparently Christmas Eve is Hannah's favorite day of the year.

Personally, if I were in Jack's shoes, I'm not sure I'd want to combine occasions. One good thing is he won't be forgetting his anniversary. Hard to forget an anniversary that's also Christmas Eve.

Just after we order our food, both our phones chime with messages.

"Message from Hannah," she says.

"I got one from Jack. He sent me your phone number."

"And Hannah sent me yours. Took them long enough, didn't it?"

"Yes. It did. I'm think we keep them in suspense a little while."

"You mean not tell them that we found each other."

"It seems like a small price to pay for leaving us hanging like that."

"I don't think it was intentional," she says, setting her phone aside. "But okay. Maybe next time they'll think things through a little better."

"My thoughts exactly."

Alice drops our ham sandwiches off and a bottle of Ketchup. "Can I get you anything else?"

We both say no.

"Good." Alice says. "I'll get those pies wrapped up for you. Sure you don't want a piece for now?

"Maybe later," I say with a glance at Olivia who's already eating her French fries. "We'll let you know about that."

"Enjoy," Alice says, leaving us to it.

"How's your sandwich?" I ask.

"Good. I haven't had a ham sandwich this good since I used to live at home with my parents. My mother made the best ham sandwiches ever."

"Will you see your family for Christmas?" I ask.

"No. They died when I was fifteen."

"Olivia. I am so sorry." And I'm such a dumbass for making assumptions when the truth is I know nothing about her. Sometimes it's hard for me to remember that not everyone had a happy childhood like mine. Even if my family does annoy me sometimes. It's easy to forget just how lucky I am.

"It's okay," she says, picking up her sandwich. "It was a long time ago and I learned at an early age to take care of myself."

We eat in silence for a few minutes.

"You're quite impressive," I say.

"How's that?" she asks with amusement.

"You've been on your own for what, five years."

"Ten."

"Okay. So you've been on your own for ten years and you're not afraid to take risks."

"What makes you think that?"

"You have your own company, for one. Mostly it's just an impression I'm getting from you."

"It's true. I don't have a lot of fear. Losing my parents as a teenager taught me that we don't have a lot of control over our ultimate fate. So I just put my all into everything I do. I figure I have everything to gain and not a lot to lose."

"Boyfriend?"

"Nothing serious. I don't do serious." She stops herself and looks down, focusing on her food. I get the impression she said more than she intended.

It fits. Losing her parents at such a young age, she would have trouble with relationships. But I'm no psychologist and it's not my business.

"Do you want a piece of pie now or do you want to wait until we get to Alpine Falls to eat with the family?"

"Definitely wait," she says. "I couldn't eat another bite right now if I had to."

"I know what you mean. This place has great food."

"Thank you for sharing it with me," she says, her eyes bright and not looking a little bit sad.

I wonder two things in this moment. I wonder if maybe bringing up her parents made her sad and her bravery is a front for something more vulnerable beneath.

And second, I wonder how she could have known that I don't share this place with a lot of people. It's sort of my own little private sanctuary for when I travel into Denver.

Chapter Eight

Olivia

I DON'T USUALLY TELL people about my parents. Madison and Hannah know, of course. But I don't go around telling random strangers.

Technically, I guess, Trenton isn't a random stranger. He's the brother of my friend's fiancé (husband).

Still. I don't know why I told him. It was more information than he needed to know over a late lunch in a quaint little diner made out of a train car.

So I do what I know how to do well. I change the direction of the conversation.

"As an architect, you must be especially able to appreciate the design of this diner. It's made out of old train cars? Or just made to look like it?"

"Yes. It really is. They took two train cars and welded them together. It's really quite fascinating."

"Is this the kind of thing you do or do you do more modern designs?"

"I can go either way. I listen to what the client wants. Try to get an image of what they must be picturing. And then I draw it up."

"Is it hard? Trying to figure out what someone else is seeing in their head?"

"They usually have pictures. In fact, I ask them to bring photos from magazines and websites of things they like."

"What's your favorite project you ever designed?"

"That's a hard question to answer."

Alice stops and picks up our empty plates. "Pie now or just to go?" she asks.

"Just to go," I say. "Thank you Alice."

"Come back and see us again," Alice says to me.

"I will." I smile, but I also can't imagine a scenario where I would be back here.

"I guess if I had to pick a favorite," Trenton says handing Alice a credit card. "It would be a small cottage I built for an older lady on a little plot of land just outside of Boulder."

"What did you like about it?"

"Like you, she liked animals. I think she had about ten cats and a couple of dogs. She wanted a courtyard in the middle so her pets could go outside. I built the house around that. A firepit and a fountain in the middle. Gas fireplaces in every room, even one in the bathroom. Very cozy."

"I think you just described my dream house."

He laughs, softening his features and sending little tingles of awareness down my spine.

When he laughs, his handsomeness becomes more approachable.

"I have photos. Not with me. But I can show you photos."

"I'd like to see them."

"Okay. I'll bring them by next time I'm in Alpine Falls."

"You don't live in Alpine Falls? At the ranch?"

"God no. I have my own place in Boulder."

"Of course," I say, wondering why I feel disappointed. I suppose I was looking forward to seeing him at the ranch while I'm there. Hannah will be busy with Jack and even though I just met him, Trenton is someone I'm comfortable being around.

"I'll be spending most of the next couple of weeks at the ranch though," he says. "It'll take me a couple of days to finish up some work at my place, pack, and drive back up there."

I bring up a mental image of the map I'd studied when I'd thought I was going to be making this drive myself.

"Giving me a ride is way out of your way, isn't it?"

"A little," he says with a little smile. "But it's okay. I'm enjoying the company."

"I hope you know how much I appreciate it. I had a

rental car reservation, but when I got there, they didn't have a car."

"Think nothing of it," he says. "You ready to get back on the road? I'd like to be there before dark."

Chapter Nine

Trenton

WHEN I TOLD Olivia I was enjoying her company, I'd been speaking from the heart. The words just sort of spilled out and honestly it was the kind of bland statement I would say to acquaintances. The problem is that as I said the words to Olivia, I realized how much I actually meant them.

With Cupcake back in her carrier and safely in the back seat, we get back on the interstate and head toward the mountains.

I put on my sunglasses to combat some of the bright sunlight we're driving toward.

Olivia doesn't seem concerned, but she seems to see everything.

"Is this your first time to Colorado?"

"Yes. My first time out west. To the mountains."

"You've never been to the mountains?"

"Never. With Houston being in the south, my friends always just sort of gravitated to the beach."

"I've never been to the beach."

"You're kidding!"

"No. I prefer the higher elevations."

"Huh. We're like total opposites."

"Maybe," I say. "We'll see how you feel about that after you've been in the mountains for a few days."

"Hannah loves it."

"Well. She's from Alpine Falls. So I'm not sure that really counts."

"True. But it counts. I think she went to the beach with us one time. She didn't care for it." Olivia pulls out her phone. "Speaking of Hannah. She's texting me again. I should probably let her know I'm still alive."

"Probably."

She sends me a smile before she answers the text.

"Okay. I told her we managed to find each other and we're on the way."

"You're a good friend."

She shrugs. "Hannah always seemed like she needed a friend, you know. Madison and I knew each other from where we grew up in Katy, but we sort of just adopted Hannah."

"Katy? Isn't that a suburb?"

"Yes. West of Houston."

"Hm. That fits." I adjust my shades and lower the visor to help combat the bright sun.

"What makes you say that?"

"You sort of have a city girl vibe, but it's different from most of the city girls I've known."

"You've known a lot of city girls?" she asks.

"No one from Houston," I say, keeping my answer purposely vague.

"Well. My grandmother had a house in Houston. I inherited it from her. So I guess I sort of grew up in Katy then lived in Houston from age fifteen."

Another piece of the puzzle falls into place.

If she inherited a house from her grandmother, that explains how she can venture out on her own. Most people seek security, but if she had an inheritance sizable enough that she got a house out of it plus whatever she would have gotten from her parents, she wouldn't have to. She would have the freedom to do whatever she wanted.

"They said your other friend Madison will be coming up, too."

"She will. She's actually more like you. It's hard to get her away from work. I think you'll like her."

"Trying to set me up?"

"No. Not unless you want me to. If you want me to, I can."

"I'm good."

And no. I do not want Olivia to set me up with her friend Madison. Not when I'm enjoying Olivia's company like I am. That just wouldn't make any sense.

I keep those thoughts to myself though. The next couple of weeks are going to be interesting to say the least. And for the first time I'm not dreading spending the two weeks leading up to Christmas at the ranch. In fact, I'm rather looking forward to them.

Chapter Ten

Olivia

I SPEND the next few minutes sitting in silence, mentally kicking myself.

Why would I offer to set Trenton up with Madison? First of all, that hadn't been where I was heading when I said they were alike. I was simply stating a fact.

I like Madison and Trenton is a lot like her so I like him, too. That had been more along my line of thinking.

But he'd jumped the other way. That told me he's not interested in dating me. Good to know. And probably for the best considering that I do technically have Stan in my life.

He deftly changes the subject, pointing out landmarks as we go.

We go through the Eisenhower Tunnel and I am officially impressed.

We take the next exit after we come out of the tunnel.

"Just for full disclosure, we could have taken the exit before the tunnel, but I thought you might like the experience of driving through it."

"I did. Thank you. Wow. It's just. Impressive."

"One point for the mountains," he says.

"You're funny. You think you're going to convert me from a beach person to a mountain person."

"You say that like you don't think it's possible."

"Anything is possible," I say. "But you're looking a life-long beach-goer. You have your work cut out for you."

"I'm not worried. The crisp mountain air will do the work for me."

"I don't doubt that. I'm not really a fan of hot weather."

"Oh. The beaches are going down."

"Are you always this sure of yourself?"

We're on a two-lane road now. A winding two-lane road with lots of trees. Some bare with no leaves. Others look like Christmas trees in the wild.

"Only when I can see that the odds are stacked in my favor."

"A betting man." I nod. "Okay. I have to keep an eye on you."

"Busted. Just whatever you do, please do not tell my mother."

"You would seriously keep something like a propensity for gambling from your mother?"

"Once you meet my mother, you'll understand."

I feel a flutter of butterflies in my stomach.

I came up here to Alpine Falls to help my friend get ready for her wedding. Not that she needs help getting ready for her small, intimate wedding, but I took the excuse to spend time with her. And if I'm honest with myself it's as much an excuse to spend Christmas with Hannah and her fiancé (husband) as it is to avoid spending Christmas with Stan and his family. Spending Christmas with Stan would only encourage him to think our relationship is heading toward marriage.

It doesn't help that I finally told him I don't want to get married.

The problem is he doesn't believe me. He seems to think he can sway me over to his side of wanting to get married. Not that he comes right out and says it. I can just tell.

At any rate, even though I came up here to spend time with Hannah, I've met a guy.

And now through circumstances outside of my control, I'm on my way to meet this guy's family.

It's all quite surreal.

And I need to keep my thoughts together.

Trenton has already made it clear to me that he's not interested in me that way.

Maybe he doesn't even like girls. He's certainly good looking. Not exactly a rugged kind of guy and he spends most of his life away from his family.

"What about your girlfriend?" I ask. "Will she be coming up to the ranch for Christmas?"

"Did Hannah tell you I have a girlfriend?" he asks.

"Hannah didn't tell me anything about you or your other brother. I was just making conversation."

"No. I don't have a girlfriend."

"Boyfriend?"

He looks at me sideways, but I can't see his eyes behind his dark sun glasses.

"I don't have a girlfriend because the last two women I dated didn't understand why I spend so much time working."

"I see. I understand that. A lot of people struggle with that." Madison for one, but I'm not bringing her up again.

"Like Madison?" he asks.

So much for that. I send him a sideways look. "Yes. Like Madison."

"What about you? You don't put yourself in that category?"

"I work plenty when I need to. But I don't have to always be doing something productive."

"I envy that quality," he says.

"Do you now? Maybe you just need to hang around someone you enjoy spending time with."

"You sound like you're speaking from experience now?" he says, turning off the highway.

We're definitely in the mountains now and the sun has dropped behind the mountains, leaving us in twilight. The sky is streaked with beautiful shades of pink.

"Wow. This sunset."

"Better than the beach?"

"Maybe."

Maybe it doesn't have so much to do with the beach versus the mountains as it has to do with the company.

"We're here," he says turning down a long dirt driveway.

Hannah hadn't been kidding when she'd said the ranch was deep in the mountains, off by itself.

Chapter Eleven

Trenton

THE DRIVE UP from Denver had gone quickly with Olivia to talk to. The travel time had passed by more quickly than I could ever remember.

"The house is huge," Olivia says, looking out of the car window at the two-story house, all the windows aglow with Christmas lights around the roof and all the windows. A Christmas tree twinkles with clear lights in the front window. "You grew up here?"

"Yes."

"This house must have inspired you to become an architect."

"Maybe. I never really considered that." I glance out at the house where I'd grown up. Maybe it was subconscious inspiration, but somewhere along the line, I started taking it for granted.

As I drive around the circle drive and park in front of the door, Hannah and Jack come outside to meet us.

Hannah runs up to the car and opens the door. Olivia gets out and the girls hug.

I open the back door and set Cupcake's carrier on the ground. Knowing she's wearing her leash, I open up the carrier and lift her out. The dog licks my hands as I set her on the ground. She runs over to Olivia, putting her front feet on her legs.

"This is Cupcake," Olivia says.

Hannah picks up the dog and gets her face licked for it.

"You'd think she's known you forever," Olivia says.

"I think she likes me," Hannah says.

"What's not to like?" Jack asks. "Hey Bro," he says to me. "Thanks for going out of your way to do this."

"It was surprisingly not a hardship." I walk around to the trunk and drag out Olivia's suitcase.

"Coming from you," Jack says. "That's saying a lot."

"Olivia is… pleasant."

Jack laughs. "I guess I should go introduce myself."

"Olivia," Hannah says, obviously overhearing that last comment. "This is Jack."

"Yes," Olivia says, giving Jack a quick hug. "I remember."

"Welcome to the Thompson Ranch."

"Thank you." Olivia looks around. "It's beautiful here."

"I told you," Hannah says. "You're going to love the mountains.

"I think I already do." Maybe I'm imagining things, but she sends me a quick glance. "Trenton is an excellent welcoming committee."

Jack looks at me. "Are we talking about the same guy?"

"Nobody asked you, Jack," I say, handing Cupcake's leash to Olivia.

"I need to take Cupcake for a walk. Hannah. Can you come with?"

"Sure. We'll be right back." Hannah gives Jack a quick kiss and the two girls walk off with an excited Cupcake leading the way.

"Do I detect an attraction here?" Jack asks me when the girls are out of earshot.

"Just being hospitable to your wife's friend," I say.

Jack runs a hand over his chin and nods. "Thank you. I appreciate it."

"Don't mention it," I say, pulling Olivia's computer bag and after a moment's hesitation, her purse, from the car, I put them over my shoulder and drag her suitcase to the front door.

Jack watches me with obvious amusement.

"Get the door, would you?" I ask.

"Sure. It's the first time I've ever known you to fall for a blonde."

I send my brother a scathing look as I set Olivia's things down in the foyer.

"Just doing what you asked me to do."

"And you're doing a fine job of it," Jack says, clapping me on the shoulder. "A fine job."

Chapter Twelve

Olivia

With Cupcake leading the way, sniffing every tree, every fallen branch, we walk along a little path that winds through the trees.

"You'd think she's been here before," I say.

"Probably smells Lucas's dog. They walk out here sometimes," Hannah says.

The dirt path is dry and firm, rocky in places. The silver bark of aspen trees contrasts with the green spruce trees that smell like Christmas. The air is light and almost painfully clean.

"So," Hannah asks. "What do you think?"

"It's beautiful here. Definitely not humid. I brought moisturizer."

"I meant about Trenton," Hannah says.

"Oh. He and Jack don't really look alike, do they?"

"Not really. Lucas and Jack look more alike. But if you watch Trenton, you'll see the resemblances."

"Different personalities."

"Jack is better with people," Hannah says.

"I don't know," I say, looking back toward the house, but the guys have gone inside. "He warms up nicely."

"You like him," Hannah says, pleased.

"No. I don't like him. I don't not like him, but he's not interested in me."

"Please tell me how exactly you know that."

I shake my head and tug gently on Cupcake's leash when she tries to circle a maple tree. "He and I are complete opposites."

"So? That doesn't mean anything."

"I think he and Madison will get along better," I say.

"Definitely not," Hannah says. "They will clash like two like magnetic poles."

"Maybe," I say, then I change the subject. "So how about you? Do you miss Houston?"

"Sometimes, sure. But Alpine Falls is home. And Jack is home."

"You look good," I decide. "Happy. And relaxed."

"I don't know about relaxed. The ranch is a LOT of work."

"What about his parents? How is it living with them?"

"Oddly enough, I don't mind. They let us do our thing and the house is big enough that we don't run over each other." She looks back toward the house, too. "It's actually kind of nice being part of a family."

"Yeah. You and I haven't done too well in that department, have we?"

"No," she says. "But for entirely different reasons. I keep thinking I should reconcile with my parents."

"If that's something you want to do, then yes. But Hannah? Do it now. While you can."

"Maybe after the wedding."

"Hannah." I take her hand. "Doesn't it make more sense to go see them before the wedding? Maybe they'd like to be here for it."

Hannah bites her bottom lip. "Maybe that's what I'm afraid of."

"Just because Theo was an ass about your family doesn't mean Jack would be. I think Jack would be supportive if your family wanted to come."

"I know he would. And you're right. He's nothing like Theo."

When Theo, Hannah's ex-fiancé, thought Hannah might be in Denver to reconcile with her family, he'd been an ass about having to accommodate them for their wedding. The joke was on him, though, because Hannah ended up reconciling with Jack and breaking up with Theo.

"Do whatever you think is right. We're all right here behind you."

"I know," Hannah says. "I'm so glad you're here."

"Me too."

"And I think you and Trenton would make a cute couple."

"Don't get ahead of yourself there," I say. "I know how you married people are. Wanting everyone around you to be married, too."

"I plead the fifth. Let's go inside," she says. "Get you settled in."

Chapter Thirteen

Trenton

MY PARENTS ARE good with people. Taking guests on horse rides every day has definitely given them lots of practice with getting along with new people.

As such, I shouldn't be surprised that they take to Olivia.

"What can I do to help?" Olivia asks as she comes back downstairs after getting settled into one of the guest rooms.

"Not a thing, Dear," Mother says. "Jack is just about to slice one of those apples pies."

"It smells delicious," Olivia says.

"You know," she says. "Trenton doesn't tell us where he gets these pies, but they're always delightful."

Olivia glances over at me. "He's a man of many secrets."

"He wants us to think that anyway," Father says.

Jack pulls the pie out of the oven and proceeds to cut it into six even slices.

"Where's Lucas?" I ask. "Out with the horses?"

"I think he went into town," Jack says.

"Girlfriend?" I ask. Our brother is usually out with the horses so it's quite unusual for him to not be around somewhere.

"Who knows," Mother says. "Lucas does whatever Lucas wants to do."

Mother puts a slice of pie in front of Father and sits down next to him.

"Have a seat, Olivia," Mother says. "Make yourself at home."

I take two plates of pie and set them down on the other side of the table.

After Hannah and Jack sit down, Olivia sits next to me. I hand her a fork.

"Thank you," she says.

"You're welcome." My gaze snags on her forest green eyes and I smile.

When she smiles back, the ground beneath me seems to shift.

It's funny because no one else seems to notice. They keep talking like nothing has changed.

But for me, having Olivia here feels like everything has changed.

I don't feel like just the third wheel around Jack and

Hannah. Or the son who's never here because he doesn't really fit in.

I realize that Hannah is saying something to me, but I missed it.

"I'm sorry, Hannah," I say, tearing my gaze away from Olivia. "I was distracted."

Hannah just smiles and repeats herself. "It's okay. I was saying that maybe you should wait until the morning to drive into Boulder."

"Yes," Mother says. "You know how dangerous these mountain roads can be at night. And you have a perfectly good room here to sleep in."

"I might do that," I say. "I've already been driving a lot today."

"Thank you for rescuing Olivia," Hannah says.

"I had a rental car reservation," Olivia says. "And now I know to get to Denver early enough to take the train."

"You don't have to take the train," Hannah says. "Next time we'll make sure Jack is there with his airplane."

"I wouldn't want to put anyone out. It was bad enough for Trenton to go to all that trouble to pick me up and drive me here."

"It wasn't any trouble," I say, taking a bite of pie and making a concerted effort not to look at her. Not when everyone is watching us. Plotting us getting together.

"So you'll stay?" Hannah asks. "Jack and I were thinking we could fire up the firepit out back."

The thought of getting to spend more time with Olivia is dangerously delicious. I should say no. I should use any excuse I can find to drive back to my place tonight. I'm going to be back here in a couple of days anyway. I always spend a couple of weeks at Christmastime here with my family. So I'll have plenty of time to spend getting know Olivia.

That's what I should do. Just go home tonight.

Distance myself from Olivia and her undeniable allure.

"Yes," I say. "I'll stay."

Chapter Fourteen

Olivia

AFTER WE HAVE PIE, Hannah and I sit on the sofa in the living room while the guys go outside to get a fire going in the firepit. His parents went upstairs to bed.

Cupcake, having discovered the fireplace, sits in front of it, fascinated by the flames.

Bandit, Hannah's Snowshoe cat, walks over and stands in my lap, rubbing his chin on my face.

"I missed you, too," I say. I kept Bandit while Hannah was up here seeking her divorce papers, but instead learning that she was still married to Jack and subsequently reconnecting with him.

It was all dreamily romantic. I scratch Bandit behind the ears and he purrs happily in response.

"What made you decide to keep Cupcake?" Hannah asks.

"I took her around to a couple of people thinking about adopting, but they didn't appreciate Cupcake's unique coloring. I think she's adorable. So. She's mine now."

"Good for you. You've been needing a dog of your own."

"Seems we both needed pets."

"Pets make a house a home," she quotes from our website.

"It really is true," I say. "The guys are coming back inside. I should bring Cupcake outside with us."

"I think Cupcake is happy where she is."

"I guess so."

Both guys are not only wearing heavy coats, they're each holding a coat in their hands.

Hannah goes right over and slides into the coat Jack holds up for her.

"We're assuming you don't have a coat," Trenton says to me.

"I have a jacket," I say.

"Well. It's cold outside. I think you might be glad you have this."

"Whose it is?" I ask, looking skeptically at the coat.

"I don't know," Trenton says. "Guests are always leaving things behind."

"I'll go up and get my jacket," I say.

"Stop it," Hannah says. "That's one of their mother's coats. She keeps extra coats around. I've never even seen her wear that one. I think it's even new."

Grinning, Trenton holds up the coat. "It's fine," he says. "Trust me."

I slide one arm into the coat, then the other.

I can't keep from getting the feeling that it would not only be easy to trust Trenton, but it would also be somewhat dangerous in one of those I could really start to like him kind of ways. Reminder to self: I have a boyfriend.

Walking alongside Trenton, we follow Hannah and Jack outside.

I know immediately that he's right about the coat. I'm glad I'm wearing the heavy coat and not my jacket.

The air has a definite bite to it.

We sit on the chairs gathered around the firepit. Hannah sits next to Jack and Trenton sits next to me.

This pairing off comes a little too naturally. I'm getting the feeling that Hannah is pleased that Trenton and I are getting along so well.

I'm also getting the feeling that I could easily fall into being comfortable with it.

"When do you think it's going to snow?" Hannah asks.

"Any day now," Jack answers. Their chairs are tucked up against each other and Hannah has her legs draped over Jack's lap.

Trenton stabs at the fire with an iron poker. "The first snowfall is always the best. After that, people start to get tired of it."

"Speak for yourself," Hannah says. "Olivia is going to love the snow."

"Have you ever seen snow?" Trenton ask, looking over at me.

"Of course I've seen snow."

"Flurries," Hannah corrects. "She's seen flurries."

"Oh. She's in for quite the treat," Jack says.

"Sometimes they get snowed in here," Trenton tells me."

"For how long?"

"Days. Weeks. Eventually someone comes around with a snowplow."

"How do they survive?" I ask, a bit aghast.

"They have an extra freezer," Hannah says. "There's never a shortage of food."

"Oh. I see." Just the mention of a possible snow or ice has the population of Houston scurrying to the grocery store to stock up on... well... everything.

"They keep a nice supply of anything you could possibly need," Trenton says. "No need to worry."

"I'm not worried," I say with a forced smile. Besides, I'm certain I'll be safely back in Houston before they get snowed in here.

"Olivia doesn't worry about much," Hannah says.

I hide a yawn behind my hand. It's been a long day, starting with an Uber to the airport early this morning.

"You know," Trenton says. "Somebody is sleepy and tomorrow is another day. Why don't I walk you to your room?"

"Okay," I say, yawning again. "I'm really sorry. It just hit me all of a sudden."

"It's okay," Trenton says. "It can take a few days to adjust to the elevation."

"Maybe that's what it is," I say. "I need to take Cupcake outside."

"I'll take her," Trenton says.

"And I need to feed her," I add.

"We've got her," Hannah says. "Go. Sleep."

"Okay," I say on another yawn.

Trenton stands up and holds out a hand.

Without even thinking, I put a hand in his and let him help me to my feet. He wraps his fingers around mine in a firm grip.

"Goodnight," I say to no one in particular.

"Goodnight," Hannah and Jack say as Trenton and I head for the back door.

By the time we get our coats off and hang them on by the back door, I'm waking up a little.

"I guess I'm a lightweight," I say.

"It's okay," Trenton says. "Getting used to the elevation takes a minute."

"I didn't notice it at first."

"Affects different people differently," he says.

"Good to know. I can take Cupcake out for her walk." The dog is still sitting in front of the fireplace, watching the flames.

"I'll take her. I don't have a dog, but I'm friendly with them."

"I got the impression you didn't like dogs."

"I like them fine," he says as we start up the stairs to the second floor.

"Just not in your car."

"It's a long story," he says. "I'll tell you about it another time."

"Another time. I'll hold you to it."

We stop at my door.

"I won't see you for a couple of days," he says. "I've got to do some things at my place in Boulder before I can be gone for the two weeks I'll be staying here. But I'll be back."

"Okay," I say with a little shrug. "Be safe." My nonchalant words don't reflect the disappointment I'm feeling on the inside.

He doesn't move. in fact, with one arm on the wall next to the door, he studies me. "I'm glad you're here."

"Me too."

Our gazes hold and I realize I don't want him to leave, not even for two days.

But then with a little smile, he turns around walks away.

I open the door to my bedroom and step inside.

Chapter Fifteen

Trenton

I WALK BACK DOWNSTAIRS, clip Cupcake's leash to her collar and, after having to practically drag her away from the fireplace, take her out front to do her business. I don't go out back where Jack and Hannah are still sitting around the firepit because I need a few minutes to think and clear my head.

Olivia, as Jack so bluntly pointed out, isn't really my type. Not that I have a type exactly. I just usually don't go for blondes.

Olivia isn't really like any other blonde I've ever known. She's more serious and responsible.

Cupcake tugs on her leash and I follow her around the

cars. She sniffs every tire before heading toward the trees to do her business.

"You're a good match for Olivia," I tell her while I wait. Cupcake ignores me.

I glance up toward the second floor where Olivia is. Her light is already out. I know exactly where her room is. Even though I don't live here anymore, I know everything about this house. Olivia made a very astute observation when she'd said this house inspired me to become an architect. It had.

Or rather my grandfather had inspired me. He and I had spent countless hours hiking along the trails and riding horses in the backcountry. He'd told me how he'd designed this house. He hadn't built it himself, but he and Grandma had designed it together. They'd sketched out a rough draft and they'd given that to an architect who had put it all together for them.

I hadn't thought about that in forever. It's one of those bittersweet memories that I keep tucked away just for myself.

I take Cupcake back inside and fill her bowl with dry kibbles that belong to my brother's black lab. She gobbles it up like a starving dog.

We hadn't talked about where Cupcake was going to sleep. I can't very well leave her down here in a strange house by herself and I don't want to disturb Olivia who is probably already asleep.

"I guess you're sleeping in my room," I tell Cupcake.

With a bowl for water in one hand and a bottle of water for me in the other, I pick up the little dog and head upstairs.

My bedroom, the same room I grew up in, is right across from Olivia's room. I take the extra pillow off the bed and lay it on the floor for her. She climbs right onto it and after turning around three times, lays down and appears to go right to sleep.

I smile to myself. Again. The little dog has some uncanny resemblances to Olivia.

I fill the bowl with water and set it next to her pillow so she can find it when she wakes up in the night.

After taking a few minutes in the bathroom to get myself ready for bed, I come back out, wearing my sleep pants and a t-shirt. I keep some basic clothes here, so I never have to worry about that when I stay over unplanned.

A spurt of alarm shoots through me when I see that Cupcake isn't on her pillow. I know I closed the bedroom door so she couldn't have gotten out.

Then I see her curled up on the foot of my bed, sound asleep.

Delighted, I laugh out loud to myself.

Chapter Sixteen

Olivia

I slept like a log through the night. Maybe I was exhausted. Maybe it's the clean, light mountain air. Whatever it was, I wake refreshed.

The feeling, however, only lasts for about half a moment before I'm overwhelmed by panic.

Cupcake.

I'm the worst mother in the history of dog mothers.

I slept like a baby and I don't even know where my dog is.

I climb out of bed, sliding my feet into my slippers. After quickly running a brush through my hair, I decide I don't look too terribly frightening.

Before I head out though, I walk to the window to see if Trenton's car is still out there. It isn't. He had been serious about leaving out early today. Feeling much better about venturing downstairs in my pajamas to look for my dog, I open the door and pad down the hallway to the stairs.

I hear Hannah's voice drifting from below. She seems so incredibly happy here. I confess I'd had my doubts about her being content here after relocating back here from Houston, but she's in the right place. I guess small town roots are very strong.

I shudder at the thought of moving back to Katy, Texas. Not a small town. Just a suburb. I have no reason to ever go back there. I'm a Houston girl now.

Hannah is sitting with Jack at the kitchen table. Several papers are spread out in front of them and she's holding a highlighter. I wonder if it has something to do with the wedding or the guided horse tours.

"Hey," I say. "Where's Cupcake?"

"I'll give you one guess," Hannah says.

I turn around and walk toward the living room. Cupcake is sitting in front of the fireplace, watching the flames.

"Cupcake," I say, walking over and picking her up. She licks my face. "You like the fireplace? Your fur is so warm."

"You're going to have to move now," Hannah says, coming up behind me. "Get her a house with a fireplace."

"Yeah right." Like that's going to happen. "Thanks for looking out for her."

"I can't take the credit," she says. "Trenton kept her."

"Kept her?"

"He thought she'd be lost in a strange place, so she spent the night in his room."

I hold Cupcake out at arm's length and look into her big chocolate brown eyes. "Cupcake. You little rascal, you."

"Jealous, much?" Hannah asks.

"No. I'm not jealous. I'm just surprised." I set Cupcake back down in front of the fireplace. And then proceed to change the subject. "So. What do we need to do today?"

"Today is a rest day for you. Jack and I have to take a family for a guided horseback ride."

"Sounds like fun."

"The horseback ride or the rest?"

"Both. The horseback ride for you and the rest for me. But I'm here if you need anything."

"We might go into town later to pick up some supplies and a few Christmas gifts. You can come with us."

"Okay. What am I supposed to do while you're out horseback riding?"

"You'll have the house to yourself. Mrs. Thompson will be leaving soon to take Mr. Thompson to a doctor's appointment in Boulder so they'll be gone most of the day."

"Is he okay? He seems like he's recovered."

"Just routine. Make yourself at home."

"I feel like I should be doing something." It's funny. I told Trenton that I didn't have to be doing something productive all the time and here I am having trouble at the thought of having nothing to do for most of the day.

I think it has something to do with being a guest in a stranger's house.

"You'll figure something out," she says. "I'm heading out to the stables to get the horses ready. Call my cell phone if you need anything."

I shoot her a look.

"If I have service, I'll answer."

"Have fun." I wave her off. "I'm going up to shower and dress."

"Good idea," she says over her shoulder.

"Alright Cupcake," I say. "You're coming upstairs to keep me company. We'll come back down and sit in front of the fire later." Taking my dog, I head back up to my room.

Chapter Seventeen

Trenton

I GOT UP EARLY, like everyone in the Thompson household, take Cupcake out for a walk and feed her.

I even have breakfast with the family before I head out. When I find myself stalling a bit, glancing toward the stairs for Olivia, I know it's time to get on the road.

Now that I'm at my house, I find that I don't have as much to do as I thought I would. Usually I find things to do in order to avoid going to my family's house in Alpine Falls. Some last minute work or some phone calls. Whatever seems urgent at the moment.

And yet I always end up going there. It's a tradition for me to spend a couple of weeks with them around Christmas and since most business offices are closed, it doesn't hurt me to take a break.

This year, however, I realize that whatever work I need to do, I can do from Alpine Falls just as easily as I can do it from my own home. So I stash everything in my briefcase, fill a suitcase with clothes, and throw it all in the car. It takes me a little bit longer than I would've liked to clean out the refrigerator and haul everything out to the garbage can. Most definitely a hard learned lesson. Throw food out before it goes bad, not after. Much more pleasant to deal with.

I stand in my apartment and look around. It's sparsely furnished even though I've lived here for over three years. Most of the time I spend here is either working at my desk or sleeping.

I can't say that it really feels like a home. It honestly feels a bit more like a remote office.

When I think of home, I think of my parents' ranch house in Alpine Falls. They have a home. And my brother, Jack, lives there with his fiancé (wife). Our other brother lives there too, sort of, but he lives in an apartment over the barn.

He's probably about as distant from the family as I am. They do see him more, though, in passing so it feels like he's around more. As far as actually doing things with the family, he doesn't do any more than I do.

Not that it's a competition.

Right now my intent has nothing to do with spending time with my family, at least not exactly. Sort of. What I *am* plotting is spending time with Olivia. So in a round about way, it is about my family.

Seeing nothing else to do in my apartment that can't either wait or be done remotely, I climb in my car and head out.

I briefly contemplate tracking down my parents who are in town for a doctor's appointment, but decide against it. They can handle themselves and it would probably just confuse them if I showed up.

Instead, I navigate traffic, making my way to the highway that will take me back to Alpine Falls.

This is probably the quickest turn around I've ever made.

My parents will be delighted that I'm there when they get back. Jack and Hannah won't care. Lucas won't even notice.

I will be free to devote all my time and attention to Olivia.

I just hope she's receptive to my attention.

If she isn't, then I have my work cut out for myself.

As I drive back along the road weaving through the mountains, I realize that I have no choice but to make this thing with Olivia work.

I've always heard that when a man knows, he knows.

And I know.

I'm going to marry Olivia.

Chapter Eighteen

Olivia

I BLAME THE ELEVATION.

Back in my room, I decide to hold off on the shower and take a much needed morning nap.

By the time I wake up, it's nearly noon and I still haven't showered.

My stomach is grumbly with hunger and I need caffeine.

I can't explain why I didn't have coffee when I was downstairs earlier. Hannah had coffee and would have gladly shown me how to work the coffee maker.

I get up and slide my feet into my slippers and don't even bother to brush my hair.

Cupcake is waiting by the bedroom door and most definitely needs to go outside for a walk.

She needs a potty break and I need coffee and food.

The house is quiet. I can tell before I even open the door and head downstairs, Cupcake leading the way. Houses have a different feel to them when they're empty. Or practically empty.

Bandit is asleep on the sofa and barely even stirs as I hook Cupcake up on her leash and step out the back door with her.

The sun is warm on my head as I walk around the back yard with her, but the wind is chilly.

The forever snow-capped mountains surrounding the area on three sides have a little cluster of wispy white clouds hovering around them.

It's quite picturesque. If I had any artistic talent at all, I'd pick up a paintbrush and paint it. Instead, I open up my phone and take some pictures.

I can hear the rushing water of the river not far from here and decide that I'll take Cupcake for a walk down to the river later. But now, we need to go back inside in search of food. And coffee.

Back inside, I unhook Cupcake's leash from her collar and she runs straight for the fireplace. Fascinating.

I don't know if she likes the warmth or if she's intrigued by the flames. Either way, Cupcake has found something to entertain herself with.

I go into the kitchen and study the fancy coffee maker sitting on the counter. The last thing I want to do is break it.

Walking into the pantry, I find a jar of instant coffee. I consider that success along with the electric tea kettle on the counter.

Within minutes, using hot water, instant coffee, and milk from the refrigerator, I have something that resembles drinkable coffee in a mug.

"You know. If you use the coffee maker, the coffee is much better."

I yelp and nearly spill coffee everywhere. Holding the mug in both hands to keep from spilling it, I look straight into Trenton's eyes.

"You aren't supposed to be here," I say, setting the mug on the kitchen island and resisting, barely, the urge to brush at my hair with my hands.

"I got finished earlier than I expected," he says with a grin. "Can I make you some real coffee? That looks rather undrinkable."

I look down at my feeble attempt using instant coffee and cold milk.

"I wouldn't say no," I say.

He goes to the counter and, taking out two mugs, proceeds to make a latte using the coffee maker.

He slides the first cup over to me, then gets to work on a second cup for himself.

"Have you had lunch?" he asks.

"No." I take a sip of the hot coffee. Wonderful. "Not yet."

"Want to go into town? Get a pizza?"

"I'm not dressed," I say, shifting from one foot to the

other. I'm so not dressed. Or showered. And my hair must look like a bird's nest.

"It's okay. I can wait."

"I need to shower."

"I can unpack while you shower."

"Okay," I say. What else can I say? He's shot down all my feeble arguments. "Thanks for taking care of Cupcake last night."

"Cupcake is no problem at all."

He's looking at me with a sideways expression and I cave, running my hands through my hair, hoping it doesn't look as awful as I imagine it must. "I'm just going to go up," I say, trying not to sound as awkward as I'm feeling. "And start getting ready. I'll be a few minutes."

"Take your time."

I feel him watching me as I walk toward the stairs. He must think there's something wrong with me still wearing my pajamas in the middle of the day.

Chapter Nineteen

Trenton

Olivia is adorable in her pajamas. And her hair, slightly mussed. She runs her hands self-consciously through it. Her features have that soft quality that comes with just waking up.

To say that I am inordinately pleased, considering that I've decided I want to marry her, is an understatement. She'll be delightful to wake up next to every morning for the rest of my life.

Of course. There is a huge chasm between where we're standing right now and getting to that point.

I busy myself with going out to the car, bringing my

things inside, and taking them up to my bedroom. I take my time unpacking and setting up my little workspace.

I usually spend several hours up here working on projects while I'm home for the holidays. It's the logical thing to do. To do my work while everyone else is doing their thing.

But this year, it's not going to happen. This year I have Olivia.

And whatever work needs to be done can quite simply wait.

I've only just met her yesterday and already she's changed my whole outlook on life. In the best possible way.

After I hear her door open, I finish up hanging my clothes in the closet and follow her downstairs.

As I near where she's sitting on the couch, I hear her talking softly and I assume she's talking to Cupcake.

But then, too late to avoid overhearing, I realize she's talking to someone on the phone.

"No," she says into the phone. "You can't. You can't come up here for Christmas. I'm staying at Hannah's in-laws' house."

I stop. Not sure if I should turn around and walk away.

"You can't just invite yourself to someone's house. Even if there aren't any rooms in town."

She sounds vexed.

"No. Stan. Just enjoy your sister. Yes. We'll do something for New Year's. I have to go. We'll talk again later."

With a sigh, she lowers the phone.

I'm feeling pretty much like an idiot right about now.

I know she'd told me she doesn't have a boyfriend.

But she definitely does. A boyfriend that she has New Year's Eve plans with. A boyfriend who wants to come out here and be with her for Christmas.

"There you are," I say, walking the rest of the way to the couch.

She looks different now. No longer wearing her pajamas. Her hair is freshly dried. She looks good. Whether she looks she just woke up or whether she looks like she's ready to go into town, she looks good.

But I have to dial things back. If she has a boyfriend, then I don't have the right to date her.

"Hey." She straightens and gives me a little smile. "Sorry I took so long."

"You didn't. I just finished unpacking."

"We can take Cupcake?" she asks.

"We have to take Cupcake."

"I just didn't know if she could go into the restaurant."

"This is Alpine Falls. Dogs are welcome."

She scratches Bandit on the head. "I guess that means you get to stay here," she tells the cat. Bandit just yawns and turns over. "I think Cupcake would be content to just stay here, too."

"We had a cat that did that one time. He spent hours watching the flames in the fireplace. His name was Bradley."

"Huh. I wonder if it's the heat or the flames."

"I guess we'll never know. I'll get our coats."

"Right. I forgot about coats. I went out earlier and it wasn't bad."

"It's a good idea to take one just in case the temperature suddenly drops. I'll be right back."

I really wish she'd told me about Stan. This changes everything.

Chapter Twenty

Olivia

TRENTON PARKS the car in a lot at one end of town and we walk down Main Street toward the Pizzeria.

I keep Cupcake on a short leash to keep her from running ahead more than a few feet.

Even in the daylight, the town is decorated with brightly colored twinkling lights. Every little shop that we pass has a Christmas tree in the window and a variety of Christmas songs spill out the doors as we pass.

There are a lot of people out. Families mostly with children of all ages from infants to teenagers.

Most people are carrying brightly colored shopping bags. Christmas shopping.

Hannah had mentioned that she wants to come into town later today for Christmas shopping.

It occurs to me that I'm going to have to get gifts for the Thompson family. I've already gotten Hannah's wedding gift from her registry, but now I've got to figure out something for the rest of the family.

I shouldn't have answered the phone when Stan called. I'd gotten downstairs before Trenton and I guess I had a weak moment.

Now I'm regretting it. He and I had agreed that we'd spend Christmas apart. Now he's changed his mind and he wants to come up here for Christmas.

I've hardly even thought about him since I left Houston. I should probably feel bad about that, but I made it clear from the outset that wasn't looking for anything serious.

He just doesn't seem to get it.

He keeps pushing for more.

"Everything okay?" Trenton asks.

"Yes." I smile over at him. "Why do you ask?"

"You seem a little preoccupied. That's all."

"There is something," I say.

"What is it?" he asks, looking a little wary.

"I need to get your parents something for Christmas. Maybe you can help me figure out what they might like."

"Oh well. I'm not going to be much help there. That's something I struggle with every year."

"It's okay," she says. "I'll ask Hannah."

"Hannah is probably the better person to help you with that."

"Maybe she can help you, too."

"Maybe."

A little girl, about three-years-old, her father right behind her, runs up to Cupcake.

"Doggie," she says, wrapping her arms around Cupcake.

"I'm so sorry," the father says, with obvious embarrassment.

"It's okay. She likes children."

The father watches helplessly as Cupcake licks his daughter's face.

"She's been eating ice cream," he says as though that explains the licking. He doesn't know that Cupcake would lick her face anyway.

"Cupcake loves ice cream," I say.

"Cupcake!" the little girl squeals.

"Come on Abigail," the father says, scooping up his daughter. "We have to let this nice couple be on their way."

"Cupcake. Doggie." Abigail starts to cry.

"You don't happen to know where I can adopt a dog like Cupcake, do you?"

"Not at this particular moment. But in my work, I sometimes come across pets who need homes. If you want to give me your name and number, I can send out some queries."

"Would you? That would be great." Abigail wiggles out of his arms and drops back down to frolic with Cupcake. Her giggling is much better than her crying.

"Sure. It's no problem."

"My name's Caleb. My sister and I run Lawson Outfitter's Supply Store just down the street. You can find me there."

"Okay. My name is Olivia and this is Trenton."

"Trenton Thompson?" he asks, turning his attention to Trenton.

"Yes."

"I've heard about you. The architect."

"That's me."

"Your parents talk about you all the time. I'm surprised we haven't met before."

"Guess you were a few years ahead of me," Trenton says, holding out a hand.

Caleb wipes his hand on his jeans before shaking hands. "I might a little sticky."

"That's okay. Cute girl."

"She's a handful. And we've got another one on the way."

"Congratulations."

"Let me see what I can find to distract this one with. Come on Abigail. Cupcake has to go home now and get something to eat."

"Ice cream."

"Yes. We just had ice cream. Let's go see if we can find your mommy."

"Mommy!"

"Yes." He looks at us. "I'll see you around. Nice to meet you both."

After they walk away, I bend down and pick Cupcake up. "Good girl. You know. He just barely missed his chance."

"What do you mean?"

"I just recently decided to keep Cupcake. I showed her around to a couple of families, but they didn't like something about her coloring."

"Their loss," Trenton says.

"Definitely." I run my hands through her fur. "She's a good dog."

"And apparently good with children. Did you know that?"

"I do now."

"Is that something you want?" he asks as we start walking again. "Children, I mean."

I'd had this conversation or one like it with Stan. I'd specifically told Stan that I do not want children. I'd also told him I don't want to get married. And yet he persists in his endeavors to push me in that direction.

But here, walking along Main Street in Alpine Falls, I feel something shifting inside me. Not a seismic shift, but something like a tiny crack. Enough though that it has me questioning everything I thought I knew about myself.

"I'm not sure," I say. "It hasn't really come up."

"I guess you still have time to figure that out," Trenton says.

"No hurry, right? Looks like we're here." I stop and look at the little Pizzeria. A big sign over the door just identifies it as "Alpine Falls Pizzeria." "Are you sure it's okay if Cupcake goes inside?"

"Everyone in Alpine Falls loves dogs."

I'm beginning to get that impression. A little town where dogs are welcome in restaurants is my kind of town.

Chapter Twenty-One

Trenton

AFTER LUNCH, we make a detour on the way to the car, to walk around the little town park. Just as I predicted, we need our coats.

"Do you think it's going to snow?" Olivia asks.

"I think it might."

"I hope so." She looks up toward the tall, jagged mountain peaks.

"Do you want me to tell you a secret?"

"Sure."

"See those clouds hovering around the mountain peaks?"

"It's hard to see the mountains for them."

"Right. Those clouds are a sign that it's snowing up there in what we call the high country."

"Right now?"

"Those are snow clouds."

She nods. "Makes sense."

"There'll be fresh snow up there when they clear. But here's the real secret. It usually means that it's going to snow down here tonight."

"Really? How cool is that."

We walk through a grove of blue spruce trees mixed with the white barked aspen trees that shed their leaves months ago.

I suppose I'm easily encouraged.

Olivia said having children hadn't come up. If she's in a serious relationship with that Stan fellow, it would have come up one way or another.

It's such a little thing, but it gives me encouragement anyway.

I don't know enough about her to make assumptions about her relationship with Stan. They could just be friends.

Friends do things together on New Year's Eve.

We reach the river and stop to sit on a wooden bench. The river's rushing water tumbles over itself.

"Cold?" I ask.

"A little. But I like it. It makes me feel alive."

"It does, doesn't it?"

The cold air looks good on her. Her face is flushed prettily and her eyes are bright.

It occurs to me as we sit there on the bench, Cupcake sitting in Olivia's lap, that Stan, whoever he is isn't here, but I am.

Olivia is here and I heard her tell Stan not to come here.

It's not much, but I'll take it.

"Do you really think you can find a dog for Caleb?" I ask.

"I don't know. Cupcake was a rescue dog, so I don't know where she came from. But maybe. I work with some larger agencies in Houston who might could help." She wraps her coat around Cupcake. "The problem, though, is getting it here."

"Jack has an airplane," I say.

She turns and looks at me. "Yes. He does."

"A dog would be a great Christmas gift for Abigail."

"Oh. Do you think he was serious? Adopting a pet is a big commitment."

"He seemed serious to me."

"We'd have to figure the cost of the flight into the adoption fee."

"Has anyone ever told you that you worry too much?"

"Me? Worry? I don't know why you would say something like that."

I just grin at her.

Olivia is an amazing woman. She has me thinking about traveling to Houston, on a private jet nonetheless, to pick up a dog for a man's daughter, people I don't even know.

Getting into the Christmas spirit is a new experience for me.

I think I'm going to like it.

I know I like her.

And that changes everything.

Maybe she has a boyfriend named Stan. Maybe she doesn't.

Either way, I am determined to enjoy her delightful company.

Chapter Twenty-Two

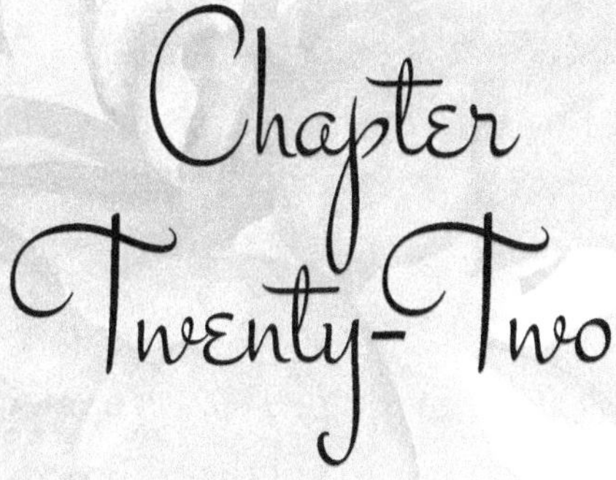

Olivia

Sitting in the little park, Cupcake barking and dashing after a chipmunk she couldn't possibly catch even if I didn't have her on a short leash, I feel a new kind of contentment settle me.

Trenton sits next to me, looking relaxed, like he has nothing else he'd rather be doing.

"Am I keeping you from work?" I ask.

"No."

"Yesterday you seemed annoyed that the holidays take

you away from your work."

"I'm making allowances."

"Allowances? What does that mean?"

"It means I'm allowing myself to take some time that doesn't involve working."

"Okay."

Cupcake runs back, giving up on her current quest to tree a chipmunk and jumps into Trenton's lap.

"I think Cupcake approves of that approach."

"Okay," he says, turning his head to keep her out of his face. "No dog kisses."

"See. I knew you don't like dogs."

"I love dogs. Loving a dog and kissing a dog are two completely different things."

I laugh. "Okay. I can't argue with that logic."

"A man has to have his limits."

"I think you're OCD."

"What makes you say that, Dr. Olivia?"

"I took psychology in college. And..." I wave a hand. "You have this thing. You don't like dog hair in your car and you don't like dogs licking you."

"Maybe you should've been a psychologist. Wait. What was your major?"

"I majored in business like everyone recommended, but I really liked the psychology classes best. I actually got a minor in it."

"Is that so? You do know that you can go back and get your degree in psychology?"

"I don't know. Maybe. I don't think I want to go back to

college. I want to grow my business."

"The pet adoption business."

"That's actually Madison's business. I'm just helping her out."

"What's your business?"

"I can't tell you. You'll laugh at me."

"Why? Is it funny? You want to be a clown?"

I shudder. "Clowns terrify me."

"Now you have to tell me what it is you really want to do."

I glance over at him, then turn back to face the lovely mountain view.

Water from the river splashes in our direction, but it evaporates before it lands on us.

"I won't laugh," he says, pulling a serious face. "But if you don't tell me, I'm going to imagine all sorts of crazy things. Like maybe you want to be an airplane mechanic."

"No. Not that," I say with a little smile. "I want to be an interior designer."

He tilts his head to the side. "What's wrong with that?"

"I have no training in it. It's a whole new field and I just told you I don't want to go back to school." I take a breath. "And you're an architect. It's sort of your field."

"It's very much my field. And I can tell you it's hard to find an interior designer who's decent to work with. I think you'd be good at it."

"I'd be competing with people who've studied it and I just don't want to go through that. That's why the pet adoption thing is working for me right now. It's low stress."

"You, Olivia, are selling yourself short. Some of the best interior designers don't have degrees. They have passion and experience. You have passion and experience just comes with time."

"People always say that. But how does someone get experience without experience?"

"They have to know someone," he says definitively.

"I don't know anyone," I say. "It's just not realistic."

"You do know someone," he says.

"Who?" I turn and look into his grayish blue eyes.

And then it hits me. I do know someone.

I know him.

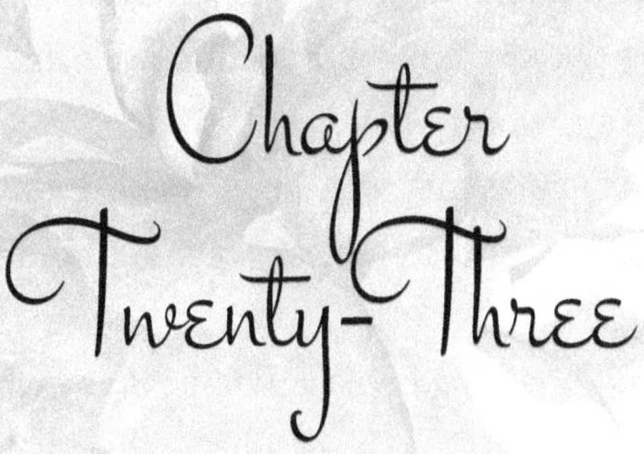

Trenton

JACK

Where are you?

I'm in town. Alpine Falls. Why?

JACK

We can't find Olivia. And she
doesn't answer her messages.

"I THINK someone's looking for you," I tell Olivia.

"Who?"

"Jack and Hannah."

"Hannah wanted me to come into town with her later." She pulls her phone from her purse and pulls a guilty expression. "I had my volume off."

"It's okay. I guess they were just worried about you."

"I'm not used to that," she says, typing a quick response on her phone.

I don't say anything because I don't know what to say. I find it incredibly sad that Olivia isn't used to having people worry about her. It was just one of those off-hand, throw away comments, something she probably didn't even intend to say, much less for me to hear.

But I did hear it.

And hearing it makes me want to change it.

Even though I know she's already texting with Hannah, I send Jack a quick message.

> She's with me.

I want them to know that she's being taken care of and that if I have my way, I'll be taking care of her from here on out.

Olivia has no family. From what I've gathered, listening to her, she has a couple of friends, Hannah and Madison, and maybe a fellow named Stan, but that's it.

Olivia is a good friend. She's here in a strange place, giving up her time to help her friend, Hannah, get ready for a wedding. A wedding in name only since Hannah's divorce never went through and she's still married to my brother.

"I told her I'm with you," she says. "I hope that's okay."

"Why wouldn't it be?"

"I don't know. You aren't really supposed to be back until tomorrow."

"It's okay. I just told Jack that you're with me."

"Oh. Okay. We're good then."

Cupcake scrambles down and sits at Olivia's feet, looking up at her with big brown eyes.

"I think Cupcake is ready to return to her place in front of the fireplace," I say.

"You might be right. She does have an affinity for it."

"Do you have a fireplace in your house?"

"No. No fireplace. Unfortunately."

"You might have to move."

"That's what Hannah says."

"You need a house with a fireplace. For Cupcake."

"I can't just move because my dog likes to sit in front of the fireplace." So she says and yet I hear doubt in her voice.

"Maybe you'll have to hire an architect to help you figure out how to install one.

"Maybe." She looks at me sideways, pulling her coat more tightly around her. "Can that be done?"

"I don't see why not. You're cold. Cupcake is shivering. We need to go." I stand up, deciding that part of my job in making sure that Olivia is cared for is making sure she stays warm.

"Maybe Cupcake needs a coat," she says.

"They sell those at Caleb's Outfitter's Store."

"Dog coats? I was joking."

"Dogs need coats, too."

"Okay. Well then. I'll have to go there and get her one."

"I'll take you by there. Do you want to go now or later?"

"Later is okay. I kind of promised Hannah I'd hang out with her. She wants to come shopping."

"You're a good friend."

"I try."

She may try, but I think it comes naturally to her.

But either way, it's a quality I admire.

She's going to fit in just fine with my family.

Chapter Twenty-Four

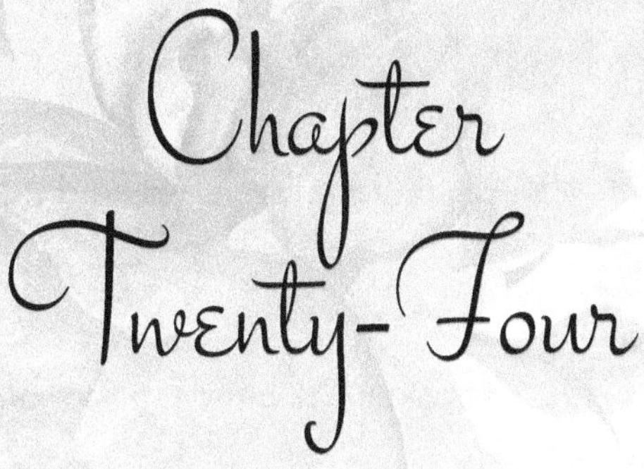

Olivia

Two hours later, I'm back in Alpine Falls, this time with Hannah. We're standing in a quaint little bookstore with wooden floors and books stacked everywhere. The building looks like it belongs in an historic district, but no one seems to notice that it's anything other than just any other store with people rushing in and out.

It has a certain charm though. A cat curled up on the counter next to the register. A fireplace in the back with three chairs in front of it.

"What are we looking for?" I ask Hannah.

"I want to get Jack's mother something light and fun to read."

"A novel."

"Yes. She's always reading nonfiction and it just seems so dull."

"Maybe she likes it."

"I know. But." She puts her hands on her hips and looks up at the row of books on one of the shelves.

"How about a cozy mystery?" I suggest. "People really get into them."

"Maybe. Like what?"

"Here's one with a cat and a dog on the cover. Can't go wrong with that."

"Seems fitting." Hannah takes the book and flips it over to read the back cover. "It's not the first in the series."

"Let me see." I read the series title then study the books on the shelves. "Here it is. First in the series."

"I should get the whole series," Hannah decides.

"Okay." I shouldn't feel annoyed. After all, I'd come up here to Alpine Falls to spend time with Hannah.

But now that I'm here, I can't stop thinking about Trenton. I can't keep myself from wanting to get Hannah to hurry up so we can meet Trenton and Jack at the Hungry Biscuit.

In and of itself, meeting the guys at a restaurant called the Hungry Biscuit has nothing to do with me wanting to hurry her up.

It has everything to do with me wanting to see Trenton again.

I'm pretty much a hopeless case at this point and I know it.

I'm just not ready to admit that to Hannah.

I help Hannah find all the books in the series, there are nine of them, and we head up to the checkout counter.

"I need to find a dog," I say. As strange as the comment sounds to most people, Hannah knows exactly what I mean.

"Here or Houston?" she asks as the young lady behind the counter rings up her books.

"Here, oddly enough. Trenton and I ran into a guy named Caleb."

"The Outfitter Store Caleb?"

"Yes. His little girl fell in love with Cupcake."

"Aw. That's too bad. He almost had his chance."

Hannah knows what it's like to decide to keep one of the pets we have up for adoption. She did that with Bandit. Just didn't put forth the effort to find him a home and she ended up adopting him herself.

"I know. But not now."

"Thank you," she tells the girl behind the counter as she takes her bag of books.

"Merry Christmas," the young lady says with a bright smile.

"Merry Christmas to you, too, Jennie." She turns her attention back to me. "You might have some luck in finding him a dog like Cupcake in Houston, but I don't know about Alpine Falls."

"I know. Trenton seems to think that Jack could help out with the transport if we can find one. I don't know if Caleb is serious enough to pay those kinds of fees."

We step outside into the chilly air.

"Trenton knows that Jack wouldn't charge him for the flight."

"Really? So that's what he meant."

"About what?" Hannah asks, amused.

"Trenton told me I worry too much."

"He's not wrong."

"Well. I didn't know. I was thinking we had to figure in the cost of the flight."

"The restaurant's right up here," Hannah says.

I walk alongside her, thankful that we're finally finished with her shopping for the evening.

"Why wouldn't he charge him?" I ask.

"First of all, it's good for business. Caleb sends tourists our way and we, of course, send people to his store. But something like that would go a long way in securing loyalty between our generations. And, besides, it's the right thing to do."

"But what about the cost of the flight?"

"You obviously don't know much about pilots."

"Obviously."

"Pilots use any excuse they can find to fly. Jack would like nothing better than getting the chance to fly the four of us down to Houston to pick up a dog."

"That's just interesting."

"You'll see. They're probably already talking about it."

"Surely not. I have to make some calls. See if anyone even has a dog."

"You will though. You'll find something."

"We're going to waive all the fees, aren't we?"

"Yep. You're getting the idea."

"How do people in Alpine Falls make any money?"

"They just do. It comes back twofold. But to be honest, most of our money comes from tourists."

Our money. Hannah has moved back to Alpine Falls in body, mind, and spirit. My friend, I realize, is never moving back to Houston.

Not that I thought she would, now that she's reunited with her high school sweetheart (and husband), but seeing her here, hearing the way she talks, it's just all so clear.

Stepping inside the Hungry Biscuit restaurant, we're greeted by a brightly colored life-sized cardboard biscuit wearing a big grin.

It's obviously a family restaurant. Packed at the moment. The scent of fried foods filling the air. I'd been told they're famous for their hamburgers and French fries. According to a handwritten note on a chalkboard sign just inside the door, they've recently added fish sandwiches to the menu.

"There they are," Hannah says, drawing my attention away from the cheerful motif.

Trenton and Jack are sitting across from each other at one of the booths at the back of the restaurant.

They both stand up as we walk in their direction. Hannah walks right up to Jack, kisses him, and slides into the booth next to him.

Trenton slides over to make room for me on his side of the booth.

"Hi," he says, his eyes smiling at me.

"Hi." I sit down next to him, suddenly feeling a little nervous.

Hannah shows Jack the books she bought, pulling them out of the shopping bag and lining them up on the table.

"Did you have fun shopping?" Trenton leans close and asks me.

"It was nice to spend time with Hannah," I say. "And the old bookstore is quite impressive."

But what I don't tell him is that I would have enjoyed my shopping trip one hundred percent better if he had been with us.

It must be the clean mountain air.

Chapter Twenty-Five

Trenton

A COUPLE OF HOURS LATER, we're back at home.

While Hannah feeds Bandit, Jack gets a fire going in the fireplace.

Olivia clips Cupcake's leash on her and she and I head outside to take her for her evening walk.

The stars are bright, scattered overhead like a million twinkling lights.

"We don't have stars like this is Houston," Olivia says. "At least not that we can see."

"Oh. That's too bad. So I'm guessing you don't know any of the constellations?"

"No. Don't hold it against me."

"I never would." I stop and look up. "The star pattern most people recognize is the Big Dipper. It's not a constellation though." I point over the trees. "It's part of the Great Bear constellation."

"I see the Big Dipper," she says. "Where's the bear?"

"You have to use your imagination. Follow the Big Dipper down for his back legs. Then over all the way to his head and down again for his front feet."

She stares in the general direction I'm pointing, but shakes her head. "I don't see it."

"Can I show you?" I ask. At her nod, I move to stand behind her. "Hold Cupcake with your left hand. Now." I take her hand and using my hand to guide hers, I point to the Big Dipper, then across. "Imagine that's a big bear walking across the sky."

"I think I sort of see it," she says.

Her hair smells like lavender and it takes all my willpower not to pull her close and wrap my arms around her.

I guide her hand down toward the bear's front legs, then his back legs.

"It's easier to see after you've seen it sketched out."

"I'll look it up," she says, looking up and turning a bit to look at me.

As she turns, her cheek brushes against mine.

"Olivia," I say, just needing to say her name.

Her lips are parted and it's the perfect moment for a first kiss.

But Cupcake races back and, making a circle around us, wraps us together in her leash, breaking the spell of the moment.

"Cupcake!" Olivia says. "She's an imp."

It takes both of us to get ourselves unwound from the dog's leash.

Olivia picks up her dog. "Cupcake, you're a very bad little dog." Cupcake just licks her face.

"She's giving you dog germs," I say.

"I know. Isn't it sweet?" She looks over at me mischievously.

"Very endearing," I say.

She'd been right when she'd pointed out my obsessive-compulsive tendencies.

Those tendencies serve me well as an architect.

But the dog germs, not so much.

"I don't think it's going to snow tonight," she says as we walk back toward the house. "The clouds are all gone."

"Yes they are. But as for the snow, we'll see. Maybe not tonight. But it won't be long. It'll snow by Christmas for sure."

"I really hope you're right. I don't want to go home without seeing snowfall."

"I don't want you to."

I don't want her to go back to Houston at all. I want this to be her home.

But that is something we're a long way from.

Chapter Twenty-Six

Olivia

THE NEXT MORNING before the sun is barely up, Cupcake hops onto the bed and barks once, obvious ready to go outside.

"Why?" I ask, rolling over, away from her. "It's too cold to get up."

She barks again.

"Okay. Fine."

I get up, but this morning, instead of going downstairs

in my pajamas, I put on jeans and a sweater, wash my face and brush my hair.

Cupcake waits patiently while I slide my feet into my boots and tighten the laces.

I give her a big hug, making her wiggle all over in delight, then we head down stairs.

Hannah, Jack, and Trenton are already up, having coffee.

"I thought I was up early," I say as I walk past the breakfast table where they're sitting.

"It is early," Hannah says. "But we're going out to cut down a Christmas tree."

"In the dark?" I ask as I put on my coat.

"We have biscuits in the oven," Jack says as though that explains everything. "Do you want coffee when you get back?"

"Sure."

By the time I get to the door, Trenton is there.

"Good morning," he says.

"Hi. My dog insisted I get up."

"Dogs will do that."

After grabbing his coat, he holds the door open for me.

There's no snow on the ground, but the air is so cold, it almost hurts to breath it in.

"It didn't snow," I say, stepping out onto the frosty ground.

"Not yet. Did you sleep well?"

"I sleep really good here for some reason."

Cupcake runs ahead and I release the slack on her leash to let her run.

"It's quiet for one," Trenton says. "And there's something about the clean air."

I take a deep breath. "I think I could get used to it."

"Be careful," he says. "There are a lot of people who come here to visit and never leave."

"I have a life in Houston." I have my house. And I have Madison and our pet adoption business. "Which reminds me. I need to make those calls today about Caleb's dog."

"I thought you were the one who doesn't like to work all the time."

"Making a little girl happy at Christmas isn't work."

"You're right. But you're also right that we should probably talk to Caleb while we're at the Outfitter's and make sure he really wants to adopt a dog. Make sure his wife is good with it."

"I think we should have gotten Cupcake's coat yesterday. She's cold."

When she comes racing back, Trenton picks her up before she can wind us up in her leash again.

"Be careful," I say, echoing his words. "A lot of people get attached to those little guys."

"Nothing wrong with that," he says. "In fact, I might have a coat she can wear. It'll be too big, but we can make it fit until we get into town."

"There might be hope for you yet," I say.

He puts an arm around my shoulders, causing my heart rate to trip up. "There's always hope, my dear."

I look over at him sideways, but he doesn't seem to notice that he just called me "dear." Knowing it's not good to read too much into such things, I don't say anything as we go inside where the house is filled with the scent of not only coffee and biscuits, but also bacon and eggs.

A good hearty breakfast for another day in the mountains.

I sigh to myself as I'm reminded that with every day I'm that much closer to having to leave here and go back to Houston.

Chapter Twenty-Seven

Trenton

M Y B R O T H E R J A C K has become quite the chef. He's a man of many talents, to say the least.

He can fly an airplane. He can ride a horse like a cowboy while leading a group of people who've never even seen a horse before on guided tours.

And since stepping up to help our aging parents run the ranch, he's become quite good in the kitchen.

After our father's accident, Mother put all her energy

into caring for him and gave the kitchen over to Jack. Everyone knows it wasn't much of a hardship for her.

No one argues when Jack claims he doesn't want anyone in his kitchen and he doesn't argue when we step up to do the dishes after he cooks. It's one of those arrangements that just sort of happened and everyone seems to be good with it.

After breakfast, I excuse myself and go into the attic where there are boxes of things no one wanted to keep lying around, but didn't want to toss.

It doesn't take me long to find what I'm looking for.

When I was a boy, I had a cocker spaniel named Spot. Spot was bigger than Cupcake, but not by a whole lot.

Her old coat is worse for wear, but it's a good warm coat that served Spot well. I take it downstairs and, since Olivia is in the shower, I manage to get Cupcake into it.

"It's too big," Jack says. "It's going to fall off of her."

"It's just for today. Until we can get to the Outfitters. I think I can use a belt to keep it from falling off."

"Olivia is going to have your hide."

"Nah. Olivia's going to be happy that her dog's warm."

"I hope you're right."

After I take the coat off Cupcake, she goes back to her spot in front of the fireplace.

"Has anyone heard from Lucas lately?"

"He's in Denver."

"Denver? Doing what?"

"I don't know. I think maybe he has a girlfriend."

"So I guess you're taking up the slack around here," I say.

"Don't I always?" Jack asks, pulling on a pair of work gloves. "Speaking of. I wouldn't turn down some help feeding the horses."

"You just want me to muck out the stalls."

"Wouldn't turn it down."

"Alright. Let's go."

Jack looks at me a moment. "I never would have guessed that Olivia would be such a good influence on you."

"I don't want to hear a word about it."

Jack holds up his hands. "Not from me. Do you even own a pair of work gloves?"

"I have absolutely no doubt that you're more than happy to provide a pair."

"You're really good at evading questions."

"And you're really good at trying to get into other people's business."

"Let's call it the cook's prerogative."

"Hannah makes you cocky," I say.

"Hannah makes me happy," Jack says. "I highly recommend marriage."

"You always did. I do remember that you got married at eighteen."

He just grins as we step outside and walk along the trail to the barn.

"Any tours today?"

"One. This afternoon. That's why we're getting the tree this morning. Hey. You should bring Olivia on the tour."

"I don't know how Olivia feels about riding a horse."

"If she's going to be staying around, she needs to get used to it."

"She say something about staying around?" I ask, trying to ignore the hope that springs inside me.

"You would be the first one to know that," he says.

"I doubt that. She and Hannah are pretty tight."

"True. But I think you would have more to do with that decision that Hannah."

I decide not to respond to that.

I don't respond because the truth is he might be right.

And even more, I hope he's right.

Chapter Twenty-Eight

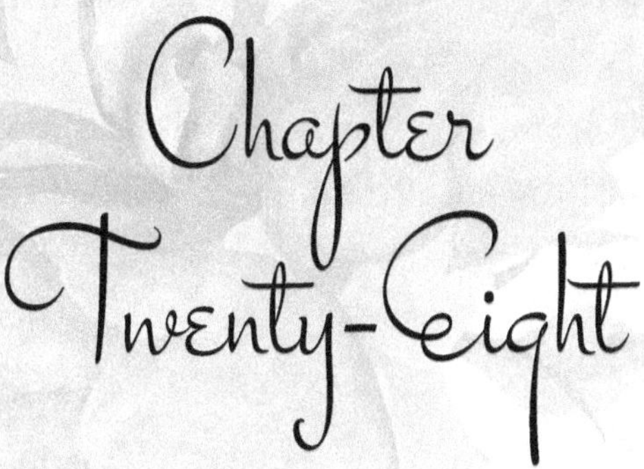

Olivia

"WHERE ARE JACK AND TRENTON?" I ask finding
Hannah downstairs, her head in her computer.

"Out mucking stalls."

"Mucking stalls?"

Hannah glances up at me. "Replacing the hay in the
horse stalls with fresh hay."

"Oh. That sounds like hard work."

"It's very hard work. Hey. Have you heard from
Madison?"

"Not lately. I'm sure she's doing whatever she does."

"I'm sure. I wonder what day she's planning on flying up."

"I don't know," I say, sitting down and looking outside at a cardinal sitting on a tree limb. "She'll be here though. In time for the wedding."

"Are you okay?" Hannah asks, closing the lid on her computer.

"Sure. Why do you ask?" I keep my gaze on the cardinal. Must be a male, I decide, with such bright red feathers.

"You look sad. Is there something you want to talk about? Is it Dan?"

"Stan," I say automatically, even though I know she knows his name is Stan. It's one of those running jokes between good friends.

"Has Stan done something?"

"No. It's not Stan," I say. "He called earlier. Wants to come up here for Christmas."

Hannah looks a little startled.

"Don't worry," I say, pulling my gaze away from the bird and looking at Hannah. "I told him no."

"If you really want him to come, we can made accommodations," she says, but I hear the worry in her voice.

"I don't," I say, squaring my shoulders. "You know how I feel about marriage, right?"

"Right."

"He's pressuring me to think about it. And if he comes up here for Christmas... for the wedding... he's just thinks he's making progress in winning me over."

"You don't want to marry Stan," Hannah says.

"No."

"Olivia," Hannah says, leaning forward and looking into my eyes. "I understand you don't want to marry Stan. But... maybe it's not marriage you're set against so much as it is Stan."

"Maybe," I say with a forced smile. "But I've always said I don't want to get married."

"I know. But it's okay to change your mind. Not saying you will, but if you ever wanted to."

"I don't think I will," I say, looking back to the window for the cardinal, but he's gone.

I sigh.

I have my reasons for not wanting to get married. And none of them have anything to do with Stan.

But sometimes I wonder. I wonder if I might change my mind if I was with someone else.

"When the guys get in from the mucking the stalls," Hannah says, obviously changing the subject to something more cheerful. "We're going out to cut down a Christmas tree."

"That sounds like fun," I say.

Sad, Hannah decides. Olivia is most definitely feeling sad about something.

Chapter Twenty-Nine

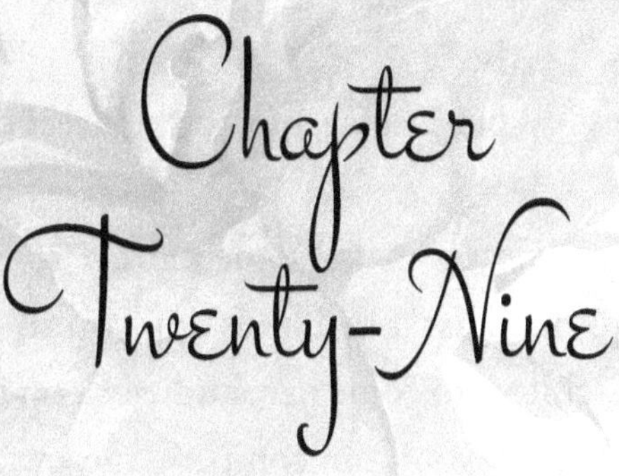

Trenton

"I feel like I need a shower," I say as we walk up the steps leading onto the back porch of the house.

"We could both use one, but might as well get that tree first." Jack glances at his watch. "I've got to get back and start lunch."

"You're a busy man, Jack," I say.

"I have a lot of people counting on me for a lot of different things."

"How do you do it? Day in and day out?"

"I don't have a choice," Jack says, pulling off his boots before going inside. I do the same. "If I don't do it, who will?"

"You should hold Lucas's feet to the fire. Get him to do more."

"Not my style to make someone do something they don't want to do. That'd be like asking you to give up your career as an architect to come here and work on the ranch."

"I don't think you can compare the two of us. I'm making a living."

"I'm just making a point."

I couldn't do it if I wanted to. I have people counting on me, too. They might not be family, but they're counting on me.

We step inside the warm house to find the girls working on the schedule.

"Where are Mom and Dad?" I ask.

"Staying in their room. Dad's wiped out after yesterday," Hannah says.

"Right."

"Jack took them up some breakfast earlier."

It always amazes me how our mother puts our father above everyone else. She is the epitome of a loving wife.

"Ready to head out?" Jack asks.

"Wait. I have something for Cupcake," I say, veering off toward the living room where I'd left the dog coat.

Cupcake is asleep in front of the fireplace.

"Cupcake," I say. Cupcake stands up and wags her tail. "Come here." She bounds toward me and this time it takes a lot less time to get her into the coat. I tighten it around her with one of my belts.

Walking with uncertainty and not a little bit of difficulty, she follows me into the kitchen.

"Cupcake is officially ready to go tree hunting," I say.

Jack shakes his head and looks away. Hannah looks horrified.

Olivia looks at her dog, then bursts out laughing.

"When you said dog coat, I pictured something else entirely," she says.

"This is just temporary. Until we can get her a coat that fits properly."

"Poor baby," Olivia says, scooping up her dog.

"Told you," Jack says.

"She likes it."

Olivia looks at me over her dog. "Cupcake is ready to go out and find a Christmas tree."

I give my brother a smug look.

"But after lunch, she wants to go into town get herself a proper coat."

"That's what we're going to do then," I say.

She puts Cupcake in my arms and heads to the back door where her own coat is hanging.

Minutes later, the four of us, along with Cupcake, are on our way outside to find the perfect Christmas tree.

Chapter Thirty

Olivia

"STAND BACK," Jack says before he lifts the axe and slams it into the blue spruce we all agreed was the perfect Christmas tree.

"We won't get in trouble for cutting down a tree?" I ask.

"Get in trouble with who?" I ask. Somehow I ended up holding Cupcake again.

"Whoever owns the land."

"No. I don't think so. We have permission."

Hannah leans over and explains. "The Thompsons own this land."

"Oh. This much?"

"The whole mountain. I think it's like maybe a million acres."

"It's not a million," Trenton says.

"Thousands?"

"Closer to that," Trenton says.

"Anyway," Hannah says. "You can walk all day and still be on their land."

"Well, that makes cutting down a tree less complicated," I say.

But for me, things are more complicated. When I first met Trenton, he didn't seem like the kind of person who came from a wealthy family.

Now that I stop and think about it, though, Jack owns an airplane and the family owns a herd of horses.

It's odd, though, because they don't have people working for them. Shouldn't the owners of a large ranch like this have staff to muck out stalls and such?

"Why don't you have a staff of employees?" I ask Trenton before I remember that it's not my business.

"Not in the budget," he says, without elaborating.

But it makes sense. The Thompsons are like me. They inherited their land just like I inherited my house. It helps, sure. But it doesn't mean they're wealthy.

Maybe having a lot of land just gives the illusion of wealth.

"Timber," Jack calls out as the tree crashes to the ground.

"All hands on deck," Trenton says, thrusting Cupcake back into my arms.

"What do I need to do?" I ask.

"Walk alongside me. Keep me company."

The two guys wrap the tree up in some kind of rope to keep it from getting damaged on the way back to the house.

I don't know how far away we are, but it probably isn't as far as it seems. I think maybe we walked around in circles for a bit as we looked at trees. There was never any doubt that we would get a blue spruce tree simply because there are about a thousand blue spruce trees on what I now know is their property.

I feel a bit like an idiot worrying about them having permission to cut down a tree.

On their own property.

But no one seems concerned and everyone seems to have forgotten that I even asked.

Walking along beside Trenton as he and Jack carry the tree over their shoulders, I get the impression that they've done this many times before.

I never had much in the way of family traditions. My grandmother did the best she could, but she was older when she took me in and had her hands full just providing for me.

She and I baked cookies on Christmas Eve and we put up her little artificial tree the day after Thanksgiving.

But this. This is different.

If I ever have children, I want to have at least two. Maybe half a dozen.

If I ever have children, I want to have a big family.

If...

Walking along the trail in the clean mountain air. Cupcake running ahead. I feel my priorities shifting.

Children.

This is the first time in my life that I even gave having children any kind of thought whatsoever.

I don't say anything. I keep these thoughts to myself.

After all, there's a very good possibility that they will pass once I'm out of this thin mountain air.

It's probably just the elevation.

Chapter Thirty-One

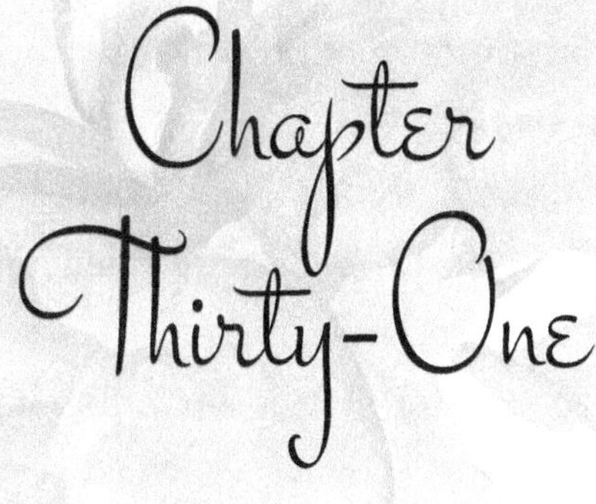

Trenton

CALEB and his wife are out when Olivia and I get to the Outfitters, so I end up sending him a text about the dog adoption.

In the meantime, Olivia tries a couple of coats on Cupcake and decides on a bright red one.

"This one does fit her better," I admit. "And it looks a lot more modern."

"Style is very important," Olivia says.

She obviously lives by this adage. After our hike into the woods, she changed into tall knee-high boots, jeans tucked inside, that would most definitely not be good for wearing out hiking in the woods.

She's wearing a red wool cap on her head that makes her look a bit like a Christmas elf, a very fetching one, and a matching red buttoned cardigan.

I give her points for getting into the Christmas spirit, especially now that she has chosen a red coat for Cupcake.

Just as we're checking out, I get a message from Caleb.

CALEB

We definitely want a dog if you can find one. Just don't tell Rachel.

Rachel is Caleb's sister and the one currently taking Olivia's credit card payment.

I look up from my phone and smile at her, trying not to look guilty.

I'm not sure what Rachel has to do with Caleb getting a dog for his daughter, but knowing Rachel, she has an opinion. Rachel has an opinion about everything.

"Do you want her to wear it or do you want it in a shopping bag?" Rachel asks about the dog coat.

"She can just wear it," Olivia says. "I think she likes it."

"What's not to like? Enjoy. And Merry Christmas."

"Merry Christmas," we both say back to her.

"Oh. Trenton?"

"Yes?" I'm surprised Rachel remembers me from school. She and I never really talked.

"Will you give Jack something for me?"

"Sure."

She slides an envelope across the counter.

"What's this?" I ask.

"Just a little refund. He overpaid for some supplies."

"Okay. Sure. Thank you."

Olivia and I step outside.

"I don't think that would ever happen in Houston," she says.

"I'm surprised it happened here. Most people would just pocket the overage and hope you didn't notice."

"I guess Hannah was right."

"What did Hannah say?" I fold the envelope and tuck it in my back pocket.

Cupcake is prancing now up the sidewalk, in her new coat. None of that awkwardness she'd initially experienced when I'd put Spot's coat on her. So much like Olivia.

"Hannah said that in the small town, good deeds come back two-fold. Or something like that."

"Caleb wants the dog," I say.

"For real?"

"He doesn't want Rachel, his sister to know. Rachel's the one who just checked us out, by the way."

"Wonder what that's about."

"Who knows. But if you can find a dog, they want it."

"I'll make some calls," she says, pulling out her phone.

"You don't have to do it right now."

"It's almost Christmas, Trenton. If I don't catch them before they close down their offices, we won't get a dog."

"Okay." I don't ask how they can close down offices when they have pets to take care of.

That is above my pay grade.

Chapter Thirty-Two

Olivia

As THE SUN starts to drop over the mountains, splashing a hundred different shades of pink across the sky, Hannah and I are hanging decorations on the Christmas tree.

Jack and Trenton should be back soon from taking a little family out on a horse ride.

"Are you still planning to have the wedding here?" I ask, looking around the living room and wondering what kind of decorating we're going to need to do next.

"Yes. Nothing big. Just family. And you and Madison,

but you're family." She hangs a solid red ball on one of the tree limbs, then moves it and hangs it a couple of inches over.

Just a sign of the nerves on her. She puts a hand on one hip. "I had an idea."

"What's that?" I ask, choosing another ball, also red, from the box and adding a hook to it.

"I think maybe we should get another tree. Have this one decorated all in red and have another one all in blue."

"Two trees?"

"Sure. Why not?" she asks.

"Are you turning into one of those crazy brides?"

"Two trees does not a crazy bride make," she says.

"No comment." I glance down at my phone resting on the coffee table. "The adoption agency is calling me back."

"Now?"

"I know. I have to take it." I grab up my phone and wander toward the kitchen, leaving Hannah with the tree decorations.

Ten minutes later, I disconnect the line and walk back to stand next to Hannah.

"They have a dog," I say.

"Oh? Wow. I didn't expect that."

"Neither did I. But. There's a catch."

"Always," she says, picking up another red ball to hang on the tree.

"We have to pick it up tomorrow."

"Why?" She looks at me, still holding the decoration.

"I don't know. It's Christmastime."

"But that doesn't make any sense. Somebody has to take care of the dog even if it is Christmas."

"Not this dog," I say, the words feeling bitter on my tongue. "They've decided to euthanize him."

Hannah sets the decoration down. "No. Not going to happen. You told them that, right?"

"I did tell her. She told me that someone has to pick the dog up tomorrow or else."

"Just get Madison to go pick him up. She can go right now."

"Good idea." I dial Madison's number. "Madison isn't picking up her phone."

"Why not?" Hannah pulls her phone out of her pocket and dials Madison's number. "Straight to voicemail."

"We have to get to Houston. We have to rescue that dog."

"Agreed."

"Do I need to look at plane tickets?"

"Not yet. Let me talk to Jack."

"Okay."

I'd been led to believe that Jack would fly us down to get the dog. That it wouldn't be a problem.

"I have to see if the plane's available," Hannah answering my unspoken question.

"I thought it was Jack's airplane."

"It is, but he sublets it sometimes."

"Oh. I'll check with the airlines. Just in case." I drop onto the sofa and start my search.

"I'm worried about Madison," Hannah says, sending Madison a message.

"I am too." I'm worried about a lot of things, including Madison, but mostly, right now, I'm worried about how to rescue the little dog.

That's what our company is all about. Not just placing pets with their forever owners, but keeping animals from unspeakable fates.

Even if Caleb didn't want the dog for his daughter, I'd still do everything I could to rescue him. I'd do it even if it wasn't my job to save him. The thought of not saving the little dog from an unspeakable fate makes me literally sick to my stomach.

Chapter Thirty-Three

Trenton

IT'S BEEN some time since I've gone horseback riding. By the time Jack and I are back at the stables and brushing down the horses, I know I'm going to be sore all over. It was worth it though, getting out, seeing some of the beautiful backcountry again.

I'd planned on taking Olivia, but she'd been doing her thing with trying to find a dog for Caleb.

Next time. Next time I go riding, I'm taking Olivia. It doesn't matter that she's never been on a horse. I have experience with that and I know how to teach her what she needs to know. We have horses specifically for inexperienced riders, so it's definitely not a problem.

Glancing out the open barn door, I'm surprised to see Hannah and Olivia walking this way. Cupcake is leading the way. The dog has an uncanny sense of guessing which way to go, even in places unfamiliar to her.

Both of the girls, Hannah and Olivia, are beautiful, but I only have eyes for Olivia.

"The girls are coming this way," I say.

Jack looks up and grins. I've never known anyone so in love as Jack is with Hannah. That he was secretly married to her for ten years without her knowing it, and never went on a single date during that time speaks volumes.

Hannah walks up to Jack, Olivia standing next to her. "We have to fly to Houston," she says.

"Okay," Jack says. "We knew that was coming."

"Tomorrow."

Jack glances at me. "Didn't expect that. Why tomorrow?"

While she tells him, I put away the horse brush and walk over to stand next to Olivia.

"Didn't know your job was this stressful," I tell her.

"It can be."

"I need to make a call," Jack says. "Make sure the airplane is available."

"Why wouldn't it be?" I ask. "It's your plane."

"I sublet it sometimes."

"Why?"

"Running a ranch is expensive," he says, pulling off his gloves and shoving them in his coat pockets. "It helps to offset expenses."

"I didn't know things were that bad," I say.

"We're handling it," Jack says, washing his hands and drying them before pulling out his phone.

With Jack and Hannah going on ahead, I lock up the barn and, walking alongside Olivia, follow behind them.

"You're not saying anything," I say.

"If Jack can't get the airplane, I have to take a commercial flight down to Houston tomorrow."

"What about Madison? Can't she pick up the dog?"

"We can't get in touch with her."

"Is she okay?"

"I don't know."

"We'll figure something out," I say.

Olivia just nods and looks straight ahead.

So now I know. When things get dire, Olivia gets quiet.

There's another possibility. Her friend, Stan.

I start to ask her about it, but decide against it. The subject of Stan isn't one I want to bring up if I can avoid it.

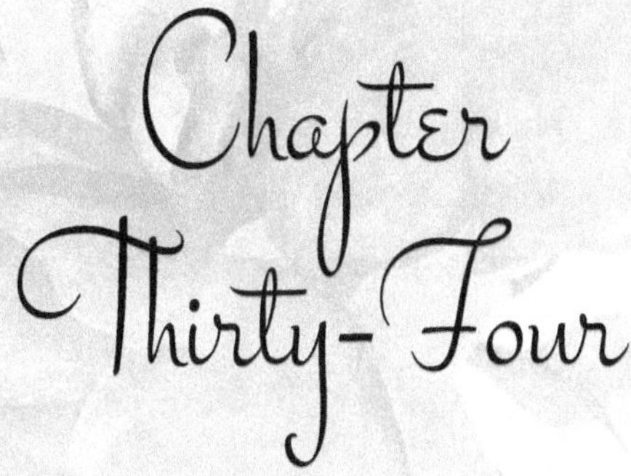

Chapter Thirty-Four

Olivia

WHILE JACK and Hannah make dinner, I sit at the kitchen table, using my computer to search the web for flights to Houston.

Trenton sits next to me, watching.

"I'm not seeing anything," I say, sitting back in the chair. "Even if we drove, we wouldn't make it to Houston in time."

"Can't you just call whoever has the dog and tell them you'll be there? Tell them to keep the dog safe?"

Olivia exchanges a glance with Hannah.

"The guy who has this particular dog isn't exactly trustworthy."

"Seriously? That's unfortunate."

"Yeah. He's not a nice person."

Hannah whispers something to Jack.

"Maybe," Jack says.

"If Jack gets the airplane," Hannah says. "We're all going."

"Either way, we'll figure something out," Trenton says.

"When did you become so optimistic?" I ask him.

"Someone has to be," he says.

And he's right about that. No one is saying much right now. I've never seen this group so quiet.

We're all just waiting on Jack's phone to ring.

Everything hinges on his airplane being available tomorrow.

I glance outside. And the weather. As Hannah pointed out, the weather has to be good for a flight out of here to be approved.

A little dog's life hangs in the balance.

If I was a writer, I'd make that my tagline for the day.

Needing something to do, I go back and try a different airline website. There has to be something.

"Will you drive me to the airport tomorrow?" I ask Trenton. "If Jack doesn't hear anything?"

"Of course. And I'll go with you. So book two seats." He pulls out his credit card and lays it on the table next to my computer.

"You don't have to do that," I say. But the truth is, I want him to go with me.

"I understand if you don't want me to go," he says. "I'm still buying your ticket."

"It's not that," I say. "I just don't want it to be an inconvenience."

"I wouldn't offer if it was an inconvenience," Trenton says.

Looking up from my computer, I meet his gaze. His grayish blue eyes lock onto mine.

"I have something I need to do," I say.

"Right now?" he asks.

"I don't know." I look away. I hadn't even realized I was saying the words out loud.

I'd been thinking how much I wanted to kiss Trenton. And that thought had led to other thoughts. Like how I need to break up with Stan once and for all.

Hannah had been right. I'm not sure just how right she is about everything, but she was right about Stan not being right for me. She hadn't come right out and said it, but the implication had been there.

I need to break up with Stan. It's never been more clear to me than it is right now, sitting here next to Trenton.

I can't be with Stan anymore. Not when Trenton makes me feel like he makes me feel.

Trenton makes me feel like a different person. He makes me feel like the kind of person who wants to move to a small town in the mountains, preferably on a horse ranch, even though I know absolutely nothing about horses.

The kind of person who wants to get married and have children.

Trenton makes me feel like a different version of myself. Maybe even a better version.

Chapter Thirty-Five

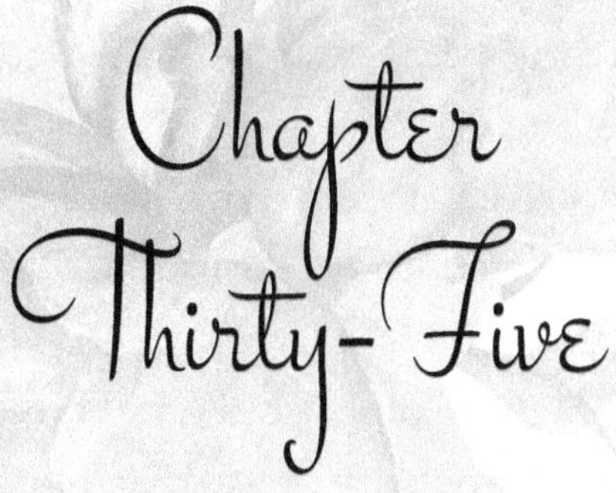

Trenton

JACK'S CALL comes in after we've all gone to bed in our respective rooms.

I know because he sends me a text.

JACK

Got the plane for tomorrow.

Elated, I stare at the message.
I have to tell Olivia.

Wearing a sleep t-shirt, I put my jeans back on and head across the hall to knock on her door.

She must have been standing at the door because she opens it immediately.

She's wearing her pajamas and her face looks freshly washed, her hair damp around the hairline.

"Jack got the airplane," I say.

"I know." She's holding her phone. Of course, I realize, belatedly, Hannah would have texted her, too.

"What time do we leave in the morning?" I ask.

"I don't know. That depends on Jack, I guess."

"I guess. We need to have time to fly to Houston. Then get wherever it is we need to go."

"The earlier the better," she says.

"I think so." I find myself distracted by her green eyes.

Neither one of us moves.

"Olivia," I say.

"I have something I need to do," she says again.

"You mentioned that." I take a step forward, closing the distance between us. "Is it something I can help you with?"

She looks perplexed for a moment, then a little amused. "I think you already have."

I gently cup her face with one hand, then, when her eyes drift closed, I lift my other hand to cup her face with both.

There is nothing I want more right now than to kiss her and only an idiot would let this moment pass without doing so.

I lower my lips toward hers until our breaths mingle.

There's no going back from this. Once I kiss her, there's no going back.

That thought crosses my mind and I know I don't want to go back.

There's only going forward.

My lips touch hers ever so slightly.

Then as she leans forward, pressing her lips more firmly against mine, I sigh and murmur. "I've been wanting to do this since the moment I first saw you." I deepen the kiss.

She wraps her arms around my waist and leans into the kiss.

She doesn't have to say anything for me to know that she feels the same way. Her kiss tells me everything I need to know.

"Olivia," I say, my lips moving against hers. "Will you be my girl?"

"I think I already am," she says.

And that is all I need to hear.

Forward. Everything is moving forward.

Maybe it's the magic of Christmas that's brought us together. Right here. Right now.

Whatever it is, I'm more than grateful.

Chapter Thirty-Six

Olivia

"ARE YOU NERVOUS?" Trenton asks the next day as we're buckled into what they tell me is a little Cessna jet.

The airfield, not big enough to be an airport by any stretch of the imagination since it's literally just a runway is near the Alpine Falls Lodge. There are no other airplane is sight. Just a couple of air socks on either side of the runway.

"No. Should I be?" I look over at Trenton, searching his expression for clues. "Jack's a good pilot, right?"

He smiles. "Of course he is. And no. You shouldn't be nervous. It's just you said this your first time on a private jet."

"It is." Hannah and Jack are sitting in the cockpit, headphones over their ears. Trenton and I are buckled into the two seats behind them. "But it should be like any other flight, right?"

"Right," he says. "It's a little bit different though."

"How so?"

"The plane is lighter, so it feels different. Especially coming out of the mountains. Sometimes there's turbulence."

"Oh." I double-check my seatbelt. "Well. I wasn't nervous."

"In reality, turbulence is nothing to worry about as long as you're buckled in."

"Good to know," I say. "Thanks for the encouragement."

He reaches over and takes my hand. "Maybe I just needed an excuse to hold your hand."

"You don't need any excuse for that," I say.

"Prepare for takeoff," Jack announces through the speakers.

"A kiss for luck?" Trenton asks.

"Looking for another excuse?" I ask.

"Always."

"Again," I say. "Not really needed."

He leans over and plants a kiss on my lips as the airplane picks up speed as the plane races down the little runway.

Trenton's lips are still on mine the moment the wheels leave the ground.

Between that first moment of weightlessness and Trenton's lips against mine, that moment is like nothing I've ever experienced.

It's overwhelmingly intoxicating.

Trenton pulls back enough that his grayish blue eyes meet mine.

We're in the air now. Jack is turning the airplane in a slow arc so that we're eventually heading east.

We are officially on our way.

The thing I notice most about the small private jet is that it's louder. Hannah and Jack can talk to each other through their headphones, but Trenton and I have to lean close to be able to hear each other. Not a hardship.

After he kissed me last night, I felt like my whole world shifted.

Like maybe that kiss breathed life into that alternate version of myself that I'd been imagining.

And now we're on our way to Houston to rescue a dog. A dog that will make a little girl's Christmas one to remember. Things couldn't be better.

Jack and Hannah will be officially remarried in just days.

My thoughts circle around and land on that thought. The wedding. I came to Alpine Falls for the wedding.

Once the wedding is over, I'll have to return to Houston to my home. To my life.

This trip, as wonderful as it is, will soon become nothing more than a memory.

And Trenton will be remembered as the man I fell in love with over the holidays.

He squeezes my hand to get my attention and kisses the palm of my hand.

This is going to be one of those memories that I remember with fondness mixed with heartbreak.

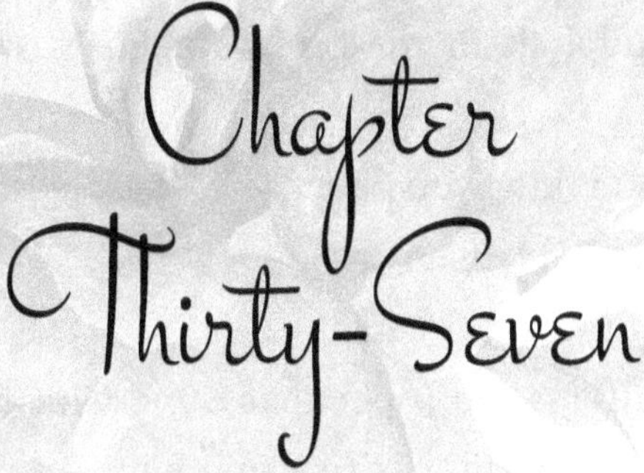

Chapter Thirty-Seven

Trenton

THE GIRLS HAD BEEN RIGHT. The man we got the dog from was not a pleasant man. An asshole if you ask me.

He made it a point to make sure we understood that we barely made it in time to save the dog's life.

There are several things I would have liked to have said in response, but I keep them to myself. This is Olivia's world and I have no business butting into it.

Besides, we got the dog.

Jack is driving with Hannah sitting in the passenger seat, the dog in her lap. "He's so cute," Hannah says.

Olivia and I sit in the back, our knees and shoulders touching.

"It's a good thing you prefer cats," Jack tells Hannah.

"I like dogs," Hannah says.

"What's his name?" I ask.

Olivia unfolds the paper that came with him. "Milo," she says. "But Abigail gets to name him. I don't think I'll even tell her about the name Milo."

"He looks a lot like Cupcake," Hannah says. "Except that his fur is all the same color."

"I can't believe that man was going to just put him down."

"I have a few thoughts about that," I say. "But I'll keep them to myself."

"We're probably all thinking them," Olivia says, putting away Milo's papers.

"Should we go by Madison's place and check on her?" Hannah asks. "While we're in Houston?"

"I don't think so," Olivia says. "Sometimes she just doesn't want to be bothered."

"I've never known her to disappear like this," Hannah says. "Have you?"

"Actually. Yes. She's okay. She's just doing her thing."

"She sounds a lot like Lucas," I say. "We should set them up."

"I don't think you want to put Lucas on anyone," Jack says.

"Lucas isn't bad," I say.

"I'm curious to meet your brother," Olivia says. "He sounds so mysterious."

"I'll have to keep an eye on you," I say. "Women flock to him."

"Really?" Hannah says, looking back at me.

"No," I say, making everyone laugh.

"We can't leave Milo alone in the car," Jack says. "Anyone besides me want to hit a drive-through for some food?"

We all agree that we do want to get some food.

"When do we take Milo over to Caleb's house?" Olivia asks.

"We can't keep him too long," Hannah says. "We'll get attached to him."

"Let me ask Caleb," I say, sending him a text.

"My bets are on Christmas Eve," Jack says. "He'll want Santa to bring the dog."

"We can take him over on Christmas Eve after Abigail goes to bed," Olivia says.

"You'll have to do it," Hannah says. "Remember that's my wedding night." She and Jack exchange a glance.

"I think Olivia and I are capable of taking care of getting Milo to his new home."

"I wonder what she'll name him," Hannah says, the little dog licking her face.

"Hannah," Olivia says. "I think you need to hand Milo over."

"I'm okay."

"She gets attached," Olivia explains.

"We all do," I say, sending Olivia a little grin and putting my arm around her.

We still have a long way to go, she and I, but I think we're making progress. Much better progress than I had expected.

Now all I have to do is to convince her to stay in Alpine Falls.

Chapter Thirty-Eight

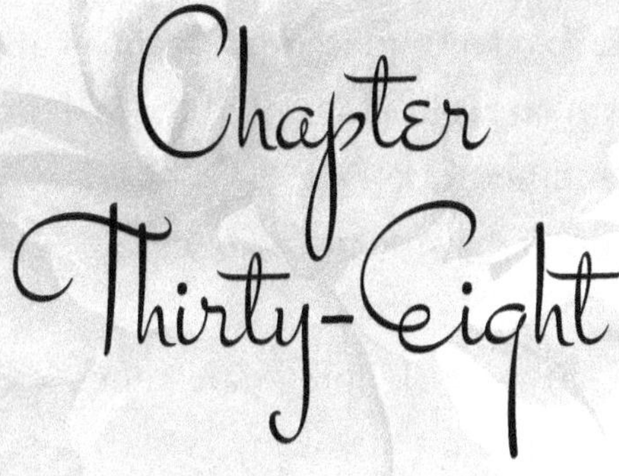

Olivia

WE MAKE it back to Alpine Falls the same day we left.

Flying by way of private jet is the only way to travel. Even knowing it's a mode of transportation outside of my financial reach, it gives me a new goal to work toward.

I find myself thinking more and more about interior design.

Trenton believes he can help me get set up and I'm inclined to believe him.

The biggest problem with going in that direction is that

Trenton can only help me in the Alpine Falls/Boulder area. Maybe Denver, but mostly Boulder.

There are so many implications wrapped up in that.

One. My home is in Houston. I have a home there. The house my grandmother left me.

Two. I don't have a place to live in Alpine Falls or Boulder.

On the plus side, I don't have much of a social life anymore in Houston. One of my two friends now lives in Alpine Falls.

Since Hannah left, I rarely see Madison. Go figure that the newest friend in our little circle would be the glue holding us together.

And of course, there's Stan.

Moving away from Houston could actually be the excuse I've been looking for to break up with Stan.

That and I seem to have a new boyfriend.

Trenton and I can't seem to keep our hands off each other.

He's holding my hand as Jack impressively lands the airplane on the little runway that looks like a postage stamp from the air.

Tomorrow. Tomorrow I'll call Stan and tell him on the phone that I can't see him anymore. It's not as good as telling him in person, but it's better than just sending a text.

Sending a text is so tempting and would be so much easier. But it doesn't seem right. Stan is a good man and he cares about me.

Just doesn't seem right.

Doesn't seem right be kissing Trenton while I'm dating Stan either.

So I'll call him.

Back at the Thompson's ranch house, Cupcake seems to think she hasn't seen me in about a year.

Mr. and Mrs. Thompson took good care of her and Bandit, too, while we were gone.

Cupcake and Milo hit it off like old friends.

"You can visit," I tell them. "But don't get attached."

"You know," Hannah says, running her hands through Bandit's fur. "I don't think puppies are out of the question."

"Oh no. I don't think Cupcake needs to go there."

"Why not?" Trenton asks. "Aren't you in the pet adoption business?"

"I'd probably end up wanting to keep them all," I say. "Anyway, I'm thinking about expanding into another direction."

"What's that?" Hannah asks.

I glance over at Trenton, kneeling front of the fireplace, getting a fire going. "Interior design."

"Interior design," Hannah says. "Where is this coming from?"

I just shrug. There are some things I can't explain. Even to my friend. Maybe especially to my friend. The friend who's getting married (is married to) the brother of the man who instigated this whole thing.

Trenton stands up and wipes his hands on his jeans. "I've asked her to come and help me out with some projects."

I look at him with a raised eyebrow. That's not exactly how I remember the conversation going.

Trenton sits down next to me. "That was my plan anyway," he says.

"I think we missed something," Hannah tells Jack.

Jack just grins and stretches his legs out. "I know you're not surprised by this, my love."

"I guess not," Hannah says. "I just thought we'd be more in the loop."

"Should we let them in the loop?" Trenton asks me.

"I'm not sure I'm in the loop," I say.

"We still have some details to work out," Trenton says.

"I'd say so," Hannah says.

"Let them figure it out," Jack tells her.

"Okay," Hannah says. Then on the next breath. "You could sell your house in Houston."

"And if I sell my house, where exactly am I supposed to live?" I ask, feeling a nervous excitement running through me.

"You could..." Hannah bites her lip. I'm not sure, but I think Jack just elbowed her.

"You could live here," Trenton says, finishing the thought Hannah started.

"I can't just move in here," I say. "Your parents can't just adopt a stray... person."

Trenton takes my hand and clasps his fingers with mine. He seems so relaxed while my blood is racing through my veins. I can almost see my life course changing direction right in front of my eyes.

"No, but I can."

"What?" I say, barely able to speak past the lump in my throat.

"I have an opening to adopt a stray."

Hannah, obviously unable to resist, jumps back into the conversation. "Adopting a... person is a serious commitment."

We all just stare at her. "What?" she asks.

"I'm not a pet."

"There might be some similarities," Jack says, backing up his fiancé (wife).

Biting my bottom lip, I look over at Trenton, and a smile tugs at my lips. I couldn't stop from smiling if I wanted to.

"There's something wrong with you people," I say.

"What people?" Trenton asks. "I don't see anyone else here."

Jack clears his throat and says something to Hannah.

"We have to go feed Bandit," Hannah says and they stand up.

"Didn't you just—?"

Trenton takes my hands. "Let them go. I need to talk to you."

After Hannah and Jack are in the kitchen, talking to each other, I meet Trenton's gaze and look into his grayish blue eyes.

"What do you want to talk to me about?" I ask. "A job?"

"The job is just an excuse," he says.

"An excuse for what?" Butterflies are racing in my stomach.

"I don't want you to go back to Houston to live."

"But that's my home. I have a house there." Even as I say the words out loud, I don't feel the conviction behind them that I would've felt before, even just a few days ago.

In truth, the thought of going back there to live leaves me feeling empty.

"If you're not ready to sell your grandmother's house, you could lease it out."

"I could do that." That's something I hadn't thought of. "But I'd have to get a place here."

"You could live here," he says.

"But... wouldn't you have to ask your parents about that?"

"Do you think I haven't already talked to them?"

"What? You talked to your parents about me?"

"We're a close family," he says with a shrug. "It would only be temporary. Until you and I can figure out what we want to do."

"You have some possibilities in mind?" I ask, the words coming out a little breathless.

"Well. I am an architect. And you need to cut your teeth doing some design work."

"What are you trying to say?"

"We have about a million acres of land here," he says with a grin. "We should be able to find a nice spot to build a house."

"Build a house? Us?"

He tucks a strand of hair behind my ear and kisses my forehead.

"Haven't you figured it out?" he asks. " I want to keep you."

"I'm not a pet," I say, feeling a little weak because I like where he's going with this.

"No. You're not a pet. But you're a person I'd like a lifetime commitment with. If you're interested."

"I might be interested," I say.

"Sounds like a strong maybe. I'm guessing you have that thing you have to do before you can say for sure."

"I do have that thing," I say, even though that thing is a definite given at this point.

He nods slowly. Hannah and Jack's laughter drifts from the kitchen. "Let's get those two married off. Officially. Then you and I can see what a future together looks like."

"Okay. But I have to tell you something."

"You can tell me anything."

"It's looking pretty good from here.

With a grin, he leans forward and kisses me.

"A definite maybe then," he says.

"Yes. A definite maybe."

Cupcake jumps up in my lap and licks Trenton on the mouth.

He closes his eyes, but lets her lick his face without recoiling.

I put the back of my hand over my mouth as I laugh. "I think Cupcake approves," I say.

"And now you know that I'll do anything for you," he says.

"Aw. Your OCD is cured," I say.

"Come here," he says, kissing me again.

Wagging her tail, Cupcake licks both our faces until we're laughing so hard it hurts.

I've found my place. My forever home.

Right here in Alpine Falls.

The End.

Keep Reading for a preview of
Forever Yours (Maybe)...

AUTHOR OF THE GRAVITY OF US
KATHRYN KALEIGH
SOMETIMES FOREVER JUST TAKES AN UNEXPECTED TURN
Forever Yours
(Maybe)
THE ALPINE FALLS (MAYBE YOURS) SERIES

Forever Yours (Maybe)
PREVIEW

Chapter 1
Madison Lane

It seemed like a good idea at the time.

That's my life. Or so it seems at this juncture in my twenty-seven years.

It seemed like a good idea to take a road trip, by myself, instead of flying to my friend's wedding. When I'd studied the map, the drive hadn't looked all that bad. Just get on Interstate 10 and head west from Houston, then north on Interstate 25 to Denver and east on Interstate 70 to Alpine Falls.

Simple enough.

It was simple enough until I got out of the car in El Paso and my cell phone fell out face down onto the concrete parking lot, smashing the screen, making it impossible for me even unlock it.

Unfortunately, of course, I lost all my phone numbers. It was quite a shock to realize that I don't have a single phone number other than my own memorized.

I don't even have my friend Hannah's address. All I know is it is somewhere in Alpine Falls, Colorado. So that's what I put in my GPS and hope for the best.

After that the trip is uneventful until I leave Denver and head into the mountains.

It's two days before Christmas Eve, Hannah's wedding date, and the weather is appropriately cloudy and gloomy for December. The forecast is calling for snow.

I don't have a lot of experience with mountain life, but I'm determined to make it to Alpine Falls before it starts snowing.

I take the designated exit off of Interstate 70 and head north along a curvy two-lane highway. It's picturesque. I have to give it that. Mountaintops covered with caps of snow. Wispy clouds hovering below the tops of those jagged mountains.

The road follows alongside a rushing mountain stream

with shallow, sparkling clear water tumbling over a rocky riverbed. And there are trees everywhere. Blue spruce trees on either side of the highway mixed with white-barked aspen trees and maple trees, both of which lost their leaves months ago.

I drive past a little cabin with smoke wafting out of the chimney sending a wave of nostalgia washing over me. I imagine a family gathered around the cozy fireplace, watching a movie or reading or just talking. The scent of fresh baked cookies fills the air. Or maybe an apple pie.

It's Christmastime and that's what families do. But not my family. My parents decided that since my brother left home, they would take advantage of the long anticipated freedom and take a cruise somewhere warm.

My brother is in Atlanta spending Christmas with his girlfriend.

And that's basically how I ended up here. Driving along a lonely country road in the mountains. Blindly following my GPS to a little town called Alpine Falls.

I could have (probably should have) stopped somewhere to get my phone replaced, but I didn't want to waste the half a day I knew it would take.

Being late for my friend's wedding is not an option. It's already taking longer to get there than I planned. Being my first road trip and all, I might have underestimated the time it takes to drive halfway across the country.

"Turn right on Birch Road in five hundred feet." The female voice of my GPS says with no uncertainty.

"Seriously?" I confess to keeping up a conversation with

my GPS since losing my cell phone. Not that it ever responds.

Since I'm at the mercy of my GPS and it's gotten me this far, I slow down and leave the highway to turn right onto Birch Road. Birch Road, a blacktopped country road, winds its way further up into the mountains. Definitely increasing in elevation.

My GPS then suggests I stop for food. Not a bad idea. Except that I don't see any signs of a town up ahead. In fact, I cross an area with a steep drop off on one side.

Beautiful, but deadly. That's what I call it.

After about a mile, I round a little curve and that's when I see the road sign. "Luchara. Elevation 8,540."

Not the population. The elevation. It's interesting how these little towns seem prouder of their elevation than they are of how many people live here.

But there's a little diner. The sign out front identifies it as "Luchara Diner." Not a very creative name, but it looks like only attracts locals. There aren't enough cars on the highway to suggest that it's much of a tourist stop.

Well, why not? My GPS brought me here, so I might as well stop. I have to go to the bathroom anyway.

I turn down the gravel road and park next to the only other vehicle near the restaurant. The town's only street is a gravel road with parking on either side. There are only a few other parked cars scattered here and there along what I guess they would call Main Street.

The restaurant is the only building labeled with a sign.

The other buildings are unidentified shops of one kind or another.

The restaurant has outdoor seating in the form of picnic tables, but it's too cold for anyone to be seated outside. The outside seating area looks quite inviting. A wooden deck with a live, very tall and old oak tree right in the middle of it, a circled bench around the perimeter of its trunk.

A little bell jingles over the door as I step inside and a man calls out to me from behind the kitchen.

"Have a seat wherever you like," he calls out in a gruff smoker's voice. The man is wearing a white apron and apparently is both the cook and the host.

Only two of the six tables are filled. A couple of bearded men in flannel shirts are seated at one of those tables. An older couple, obviously tourists from the way they're dressed are seated at the other one. He's wearing slacks and a polo shirt. She's wearing a casual dress and sandals.

I take a seat next to the door and pick up the sheet of paper that serves as a menu. Not a lot of variety. Everything has eggs in one form or another.

The man comes to stand next to me.

"That's the breakfast menu," he says, looking over my shoulder. "You can order from it if you want to, but this here is the lunch menu." He hands me another piece of paper with items that sound a lot more like lunch items. Hamburgers. French fries. A fried chicken plate.

"Can I get a hamburger? Well done?" I ask.

"Sure thing. Anything to drink?"

I hold up a bottle of water I brought in with me. "I'm good."

"Suit yourself. Got bottles of beer if you change your mind."

"I'll keep that in mind."

The cook/server leaves me alone at the table and heads back behind the counter to the kitchen.

The men laugh loudly at something one of them said.

I tap my fingers on the table. Without a cell phone, I have pretty much nothing to do to entertain myself.

I'm certain my friend Hannah and Olivia have tried to reach me by now. Hannah will be concerned that I'm not answering my phone, but Olivia, whom I've known since grade school, will think I'm just in one of my work mode periods.

I do that sometimes. I close myself off in my apartment and don't want to talk to anyone.

I might be introverted. But it's the only way I know to get everything done.

Right now I'm trying to start a business and it's not going like it's supposed to.

I literally have my life planned out on a spreadsheet. I'm twenty-five now and I'm supposed to have gotten my business off the ground by now.

It might be time for a pivot.

Fortunately, I have contingencies built into my spreadsheet.

It's definitely time to rearrange some things.

My hamburger and fries arrive. Finally. One thing I've

discovered is that eating at restaurants alone without a cell phone is not fun. There's not only not anyone to talk to, but there's nothing to read or watch.

My first order of business after I make it to Alpine Falls is to get my cell phone replaced. I just have to get there first. To let them know I'm okay and that I'm not going to miss the wedding.

The wedding is a long story, but it's important to Hannah.

She's marrying her high school sweetheart Jack Thompson.

The funny thing about it is she spent the last ten years thinking she and Jack were divorced when in fact, they've been married all this time.

So technically Jack is already her husband, not her fiancé.

But since Hannah dated other guys and was actually engaged to someone else when she learned that she was still married to Jack, they feel like they should have a wedding to reset their marriage.

Personally, I think it's a good idea.

The hamburger isn't bad. I eat half of it and all my fries before going up to the counter to pay. Now that I've eaten, I'm ready to get going. I should be in Alpine Falls by the end of the day if my GPS is correct and I'm ready.

I'm wishing I could just fly home after the wedding, but, of course, I have my car.

Again. It seemed like a good idea at the time.

Forever Yours (Maybe)

PREVIEW

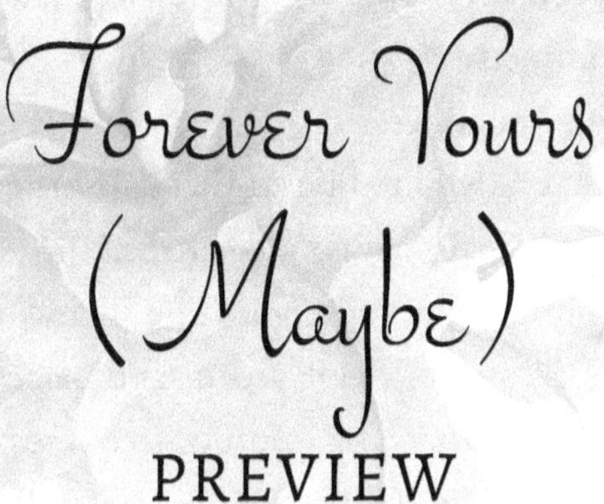

Chapter 2
Lucas Thompson

I lock the door to the cabin and walk the distance to the Luchara Diner. It only takes me fifteen minutes to get there, door to door. My big gangly black lab, Scout, runs along at my heels.

The old log cabin built in the last century is perfectly

located for someone who cherishes privacy. A writer maybe. Or a retired couple. Maybe an investor who wants to rent it out in the summers.

So many possibilities.

The air has a definite bite to it and I shrug deeper into my fleece-lined coat. My boots crunch on frosty snow protected from the day's sunlight. The trail winds among a variety of trees, most of them, aspens and maples, with bare winter branches. Others, blue spruce trees mostly, have full branches that smell like Christmas.

I automatically glance at my watch. Two days before Christmas Eve. Two days before my brother's wedding. Tomorrow I need pack up and make the short drive back to Alpine Falls.

I have little doubt that they've been trying to reach me, but since there's no cell phone service in Luchara, I wouldn't know.

Fortunately, since I have a habit of disappearing for weeks at the time, they don't expect much out of me. I established that habit during my party days. I never predicted that bad habit established in my college years would serve me well in the future. This time I have a legitimate reason for being off by myself.

As I near the diner, a police car pulls up and parks between two tourist's cars.

Luchara doesn't get very many visits by the police, certainly not state troopers. Either something happened or the policeman is just passing through. Luchara is a quiet little community. Another thing that makes it attractive.

That and it's just half an hour's drive from Alpine Falls.

The bell rings as I go inside the diner.

Mel is standing behind the counter, hands on his hips. The state police officer drags off his sun glasses and says something I can't hear.

There's a young lady standing at the counter, credit card in hand, waiting to pay.

The only other people in the diner are two loggers working in the area and an older touristy couple. Everyone is quietly watching the interaction between Mel and the policeman.

I walk up and lean an elbow on the counter. It has the desired effect. Both men look at me. Scout sits down behind me, but no one notices him.

"Everything okay?" I ask with my disarming expression that makes it hard for most people to admonish me for interrupting.

"No," Mel says in his gruff smoker's voice. He doesn't smoke anymore, but the gruffness stuck even after he quit. "There was an avalanche on Birch Road."

My gut twists. Birch Road is the only way to get from here back to the highway. I'm honestly surprised I didn't hear the avalanche. Was probably running the power saw when it happened.

"Anybody hurt?" I ask.

"Don't think so," the policeman says. "But the road is going to be blocked indefinitely."

"Wait," the young lady jumps in. I immediately detect a distinct southern drawl. She has the same accent as Olivia, a friend of my brother's fiancé/wife. Not from here. "I have to get to Alpine Falls."

"Not going to happen," the policeman says with nothing more than a halfway glance in her direction. "The road was washed off the side of the mountain."

She's shaking her head, but the policeman is talking to Mel again. "Make a list of supplies you're going to need. I'll make they get helicoptered in."

"How are you getting out?" I ask the policeman.

"I'm not. No one is getting out." He looks at Mel again. "I hope you have a room for these people."

"The loggers have a trailer," Mel says. He nods in the direction of the older couple. "They're staying at the B&B. No other guests."

I look at the woman waiting to pay for her food. She crosses her arms.

She looks like a vexed elfin princess. Delicate features. Long brunette hair pulled back loosely, leaving a few strands framing her face.

Long dark eyelashes and the greenest eyes I've ever seen. Green like a lush verdant forest after a rain.

"I don't know where you're going to sleep," Mel says to the policeman, ignoring her.

"Hoping you have an extra room."

Mel sighs. "We'll figure something out."

"What about her?" The policeman asks, finally acknowledging the young lady's presence.

Everyone is looking at the young lady now.

"I can't stay here," she says, with a stubborn lift of her chin.

"Lady," the policeman says. "Unless you're planning on hiking out of here, which I don't recommend with the snow coming, you're not going anywhere."

"She can stay in my cabin," I say, blurting out the words before I have time to think about just how impossible that will be.

Chapter 3
Madison

"I guess everything is settled then," Mel, the cook and apparently the owner of this diner, says.

"I don't think so," I say, sliding my credit card into my coat pocket. Right now I have more important things to worry about than paying for a ten dollar meal.

Mel turns back to the stove and flips a burger while the policeman turns and walks outside, murmuring something into his radio.

With nothing left to do but to address the man who just offered me his cabin in the midst of this unfortunate event, I turn to face him.

He looks like he hasn't shaved in a couple of days, but beneath that stubble is a handsome man. A breathtakingly handsome man with steel blue eyes pinned on mine.

"I can't stay in your cabin," I say.

"Suit yourself," he says with a little shrug.

"I have to get to Alpine Falls."

"Don't we all?" he says, signaling Mel. Mel throws together a hamburger, scoops up some fries, and slides the plate over to the man. He follows that up with a cold bottle of beer.

The man takes the plate and the beer to the nearest table and sits down to eat.

I'm at a loss. Stranded.

"Aren't there any rooms here?" I ask Mel. "There has to be someplace I can stay."

"Sorry ma'am. We have two rooms in town and they're both taken."

"What about your place?"

"Oh no," Mel says with a glance toward the policeman standing outside. "I've already got one unwanted guest in my one bedroom house. My wife is already going to kill me."

"Well," I say, looking over at the man who offered his cabin. "I don't know that man."

"Name's Lucas. I reckon he doesn't know you either."

Mel makes a good point. I glance over my shoulder at Lucas. He seems to have forgotten about me.

"I need to pay for my food," I say, sounding as weary as I feel.

Mel sends me a look that I interpret as him really not wanting to be bothered with ringing up my burger. Like everyone else, he suddenly has far more important things to think about.

If the avalanche washed out the road and snow is on the way, it could be spring before we have a way out of here.

I need to sit down.

I just drove over that road. Birch Road.

The avalanche could have so easily have happened as I was driving up here.

"Ten dollars even," Mel says.

I don't question him. Maybe there are no taxes here. Not seeing any place to scan my card, I hand it over to him. He places it on a little machine and manually makes an imprint of it. Then hands me a piece of paper to sign. I haven't seen one of these since I was a kid.

I sign it and hand it back.

"Is there some place in town where I can buy a cell phone?"

"A cell phone?" He scoffs. "We don't even have cell phone service here. Why would anyone try to sell a cell phone?"

"Has this ever happened before?" I ask him. "An avalanche?"

"Lady," he says. "As much as I'd like to stop and chat." He obviously does not want to chat with me. "I don't have the time. If you have any sense at all, you'll go over and introduce yourself to Lucas. He's your best bet right now and unless you want to take up sleeping in your car, you'll make nice with him."

I walk over to where Lucas is finishing up his burger and fries and drinking his beer.

"Hi," I say. "I'm Madison."

"I'm Lucas," he says, his expression blank, wiping his hands on a napkin.

"You said you have a cabin I can rent for until we can get out of here?"

"The offer stands," he says, pushing his plate away.

"I didn't mean to offend you. I was just..." Looking away, I tuck a strand of hair behind an ear. Asking for favors is not one of my strengths. But he did offer. "Well. I was caught off guard."

"We're all a little caught off guard right now."

"Have this ever happened before?" I ask. "Just wondering how long we're going to be stuck here."

"It happens in the mountains. But it hasn't happened here. It could be a year before they have a road open again. Depends on the engineers."

My jaw drops along with my stomach. "A year?" I drop into the seat across from him. "Surely not."

"I'll walk down there tomorrow and take a look."

"Can I go?"

"Do you have hiking boots?"

"No."

"Then it's not a good idea." He pulls a treat out of his pocket and hands it to his dog. The dog sets it down at his feet and looks at me with big brown eyes.

"You have a dog," I say as though I just now noticed. "In a restaurant."

Lucas hesitates a moment as though he can't quite decide if he's supposed to provide an explanation. Finally he simply says. "His name is Scout."

"Scout." I slide out of my chair and kneel in front of the dog, holding out a hand for him to sniff. "Hi Scout. I'm Madison."

The dog licks my hand, then stands up and wags his tail, letting me pet him.

At least I've found one positive thing in the little community of Lachara. A friendly black lab.

As for what I'm going to do about being stranded here is another matter entirely.

No way out of here. My trusty GPS sent me into an impossible situation.

No cell phone and I don't have phone numbers to call my friends.

No place to stay unless I stay in Lucas's cabin.

Forever Yours (Maybe)

PREVIEW

Chapter 4
Lucas

While scarfing down my burger and fries, my thoughts are racing.

The avalanche changes everything, especially if it's as bad as the state trooper suggested. It's bad enough that the officer isn't able to get out, so there's that. I'll hike down at some point and take a look for myself, but I'm not optimistic.

The timing is the worst. I'd been planning on leaving here tomorrow. I should have left today, but that's tricky because leaving today, I could have been caught in the avalanche.

I'm so close to getting the outside of the cabin finished. If I don't get it finished before the snow settles in, it'll be spring. So I might as well resign myself to going ahead and moving to the inside renovations. This sets me back a bit, but not a lot and...

"Hi." I look up to find the young lady I'd seen standing at the counter now standing at my table. "I'm Madison," she says with a tentative smile.

"Lucas," I say.

I'm not from the south, but my mother, having grown up in the south, drilled being a gentleman into my head. My brothers and I all got a steady dose of how to treat a lady.

There's no way I could just leave a damsel in distress standing there. On the flip side, I'm not going to force my help onto someone who doesn't want it. I blame our independent mother for that one, too.

In the heat of the moment, as a gentleman, I'd offered for her to stay in my cabin. I'm quite familiar with Luchara and there really isn't anywhere else for her to crash.

Luchara is a small town community with a population of 65. There's not even a sheriff.

It's not a tourist town. Just a little community of people who live thirty minutes from Alpine Falls. There are all of two rentable rooms and they're obviously occupied at the moment.

And now we're all stranded for God knows how long.

My cabin is in no way whatsoever set up to have someone staying there. There's not even a bed. I'm sleeping on the floor in what can only be described as a construction zone.

But I do have heat and running water and electricity. So there is that.

Now that I've made the offer, I can't very well go back on it.

Besides, Scout obviously approves. In fact, he's making a fool of himself over her.

"I hope you don't mind dog germs," I say, thinking about my brother, Trenton, who likes dogs well enough as long as they don't lick his face.

"I'm friendly with them," Madison says, looking up at me with a happy grin on her face. "I don't have anywhere else to go," she says. "So thank you for letting me stay in your cabin."

"You might change your mind when you see it," I say. "I should warn you it's under construction."

"From what I'm told, it's my only option."

"Okay then," I say. "Did you already eat?"

"Yes. I was just about to leave."

"Good. The cabin doesn't have any food or a stove."

"Sounds like my kind of place."

I look at her sideways and wonder if maybe she misunderstood me. I decide to let it go. When she sees the cabin, she may decide that sleeping in her car isn't such a bad option after all.

Luchara does have a little gas pump hidden behind what passes for a General Store so if she decide to do something crazy like that, she'd at least have plenty of fuel.

"We should get you settled in then," I say.

"Okay." She stands up and secures her scarf around her neck. "I'm parked just outside."

"We walked," I say. "It's not far, so just follow us."

"Do you want to ride?" she asks.

"No. We'll walk. Scout has a propensity to shed and lick car windows."

"I don't mind dog hairs," she says.

"It's seriously not far," I say.

She shrugs. "Okay."

The little bell rings overhead as we step outside. It feels like it's dropped twenty degrees since I walked into the diner.

I hold onto Scout's collar and watch as she gets into her car.

We start walking ahead as she backs out.

I can't help but wonder what I've gone and done.

The cabin is so far from ready to have anyone other than me seeing it, much less staying in it.

I'm going to need to cut some firewood to make sure it's warm. And I'm going to need to come back and buy some more blankets and a pillow while she settles in.

The cabin is tucked deep in the trees sitting on the edge of the river. At night, the sounds of the river drift through the windows like a lullaby—one of the things that initially attracted me to the cabin.

Two sets of sawhorses are out front, a stack of lumber near them. Another stack of logs that I'm using to give the outside wall a refresh isn't far away.

While I wait for Madison to park her car, I pick up the power saw I left outside when I went to lunch and stash it in metal storage crate in the back of my truck.

"This is it," I say as she gets out of her car. "I warned you. It's a work in progress."

"I don't mind. It's in a beautiful location," she says, closing her door. "The river sounds like a water fountain."

"Makes for good sleeping," I say. "Want help with your luggage?"

"Sure," she says. "I have an overnight bag in the back seat."

"Computer?" I ask.

"Didn't bring one," she says. "I don't have a laptop."

"Sometimes it's nice to take a break from technology."

"Sometimes that just happens," she says. "whether you want it to or not."

As I toss her overnight bag over my shoulder, Scout runs excited circles around her.

"He's just a puppy," she says, smiling.

"Yeah. Not sure how old he is. He was a stray."

"Aw. That makes me appreciate him—and you—even more."

Those little words of praise have me puffing out my

chest with pride. I like it that I did something that pleases this girl.

I push open the door and let her walk in first.

"I feel like I should apologize for the state of the cabin, but it has heat and running water and electricity."

"No need to apologize," she says, stepping over a two by four lying in the floor.

"I need to pick up these hazards. Wasn't expecting company."

She walks to the bedroom door. Peeks inside.

The she turns around and faces me. "I don't see a bed," she says.

"There's no bed. But I'll light a fire and you can sleep on the floor. It'll be cozy."

"Cozy is good."

"I'm just going to put your bag over here on this counter."

"Thank you so much," she says.

"Don't mention it. I'll let you get settled in. I'm just going out to chop some firewood."

"Okay. Do you live nearby?"

"Not exactly," I say. "I'm stranded here. Like you."

She tilts her head and looks at me. "What do you mean?"

"I'm staying here, too. In the cabin."

Keep Reading Forever Yours (Maybe)...

ALSO BY KATHRYN KALEIGH

CONTEMPORARY

The Gravity of Us Series

(Reading Order)

Just Breathe

Just Surface

Just Melt

Standalone Suspense

Out of Ashes

Alpine Falls (Maybe Yours) Series

(Reading Order)

Still Yours (Maybe)

Yours for Christmas (Maybe)

Forever Yours (Maybe)

(ALPINE FALLS)

Stranded in Alpine Falls

Belonging in Alpine Falls

The Spirit of Christmas in Alpine Falls

Christmas Wishes in Alpine Falls

Finding True North in Alpine Falls

A Ghost of Christmas Magic in Alpine Falls

Secrets and Second Chances

Honeymoon with a Stranger

Not Our Wedding

(SILVER PINES)

The Way Back to You

Back to Where We Began

When We Were Us

(ONCE UPON FOREVER)

My Forever Guy

Our Forever Love

Forever Vows

Finding Forever

Accidentally Forever

(TRUE NORTH)

Borrowed Until Monday

Still Mine

The Moon and the Stars at Christmas

Perfectly Mismatched

On the Way to Forever

A Merry Little Christmas

On the Way Home to Christmas

It was Always You

(UNBREAK MY HEART)

Begin Again

Love Again

Falling Again

(FOR THE LOVE OF THE FLIGHT)

Just Stay

Just Chance

Just Believe

Just Us

Just Once

Just Happened

Just Maybe

Just Pretend

Just Because

(MAGNETIC NORTH)

Second Chance Kisses

Second Chance Secrets

First Time Charm

Three Broken Rules

Second Chance Destiny

Unexpected Vows

(FALLING FOR CHRISTMAS)

The Heart of Christmas

The Magic of Christmas

In a One Horse Open Sleigh

A Secret Royal Christmas

An Old Fashioned Christmas

(CITY SKYLINE BILLIONAIRES)

Billionaire's Unexpected Landing

Billionaire's Accidental Girlfriend

Billionaire's Fallen Angel

Billionaire's Secret Crush

Billionaire's Barefoot Bride

(TRULY, MADLY, DEEPLY)

The Lady in the Red Dress

On the Edge of Chance

Sealed with a Kiss

Kiss Me at Midnight

The Heart Knows

(STOLEN ECHOES)

When Cupid's Arrow Strikes

Chasing Fireflies

A Chance Encounter

(EDGE OF THE HORIZON)

The Forever Equation

Pretend Boyfriend

All our Tomorrows

Kissing for Keeps

Out of the Blue

The Princess and the Playboy

(RED LIPSTICK KISSES)

Red Lipstick Kisses and Small Town Wishes

Stolen Dances and Big City Chances

Chance Connections and Upside Down Plans

A Christmas Kiss on the Twenty-Fifth

Believe in the Magic of Christmas

Vows of Inheritance Series

(Reading Order)

Vow to Protect

Vow to Redeem

ROMANTASY

(IN THE SPIRIT OF LOVE)

Spirits of the Heart

Out of Dreams and Ashes

Etched Upon the Heart

WESTERN ROMANCE

(LONE STAR HEARTS)

Wanted by a Texas Ranger

Saved by a Texas Ranger

(WHISKEY SPRINGS)

Finding Natalie

Promising Samantha

Falling for Allyson

Saving Savannah

Claiming Charlie

Rescuing Keira

Protecting Gabriella

Courting Isabella

TIME TRAVEL

(INTO THE MIST)

Written in the Wind

Scripted in the Stars

Destined in the Twilight

Promised in the Mist

Trapped in the Melody

(DRAGON'S BLOOD)

Dragon's Blood

Lavender Blue

Champagne Silver

Twilight Frost

Mountbatten Pink

(WHEN HEARTSTRINGS BECKON)

Rescued in Time

Meet me in 1879

(WHEN HEARTSTRINGS ECHO)

Messages Across Time

Falling Through to Forever

Once Upon a Winter's Spell

(BECKONED)

Before the Storm

Twist of Fate

When the Stars Align

Once Upon a Christmas

Once in a Blue Moon

A Wish Upon a Star

(BEGUILED)

When Lightning Strikes

Storm of Time

Midnight Storm

When the Moon Falls

Stormborn Angel

(SPELLED)
Time Tempest
The Heart Remembers
A Moment in Time
Moonlight Shadows

HISTORICAL

(TAPESTRY OF BLUE AND GRAY)
Shadows Beneath Magnolia Blooms
Secrets Among Southern Roses

(IT HAPPENED BY ACCIDENT)
Accidentally Alluring
Accidentally Married

(SOUTHERN BELLE CIVIL WAR)
Beyond Enemy Lines
Love Always
Hearts Under Siege
Hearts Under Fire
Away Down South in Dixie
The Reluctant Bride
Stay with Me
Jasmine Kisses

Magnolia Kisses

Gardenia Kisses

(THE QUINNS)

Wait for Me

Take Me Home

Keep Me Safe

FATED MATES

Riley's Mate

Aiden's Mate

Brayden's Mate

STANDALONE SUSPENSE

Lost and Found

All I Want for Christmas

Serenity

Courting Alley Cat

All of the books in each Series are standalone and can be read out of order. However, some books have characters from the previous stories in them.

Sign up for my NEWSLETTER to get all my romance releases, sales, Kickstarter announcements, and a **FREE** romance, SEALED WITH A KISS